SWIFTOPIA

Swiftopia

Ryan Starbloak

Cover art by Anna Kira

Edited by Rogena Mitchell-Jones

Visit my website at:
www.ryansleavitt.com/starbloak

Also by Ryan Starbloak:

Freckles Over Scars
GOD & everything
First Reality
This Never Happened Somewhere
Funny Looks On a Serious Face
The Alternative Wrong

As Ryan S. Leavitt:

Writer, Seeker, Killer

THE FELLED
Never Going Back
Pure Intention

Frenchmen
ART & BOOKS
New Orleans

Table of Contents

To Nicole, my most favorite swiftie.

"There is nothing I do better than revenge"
-Taylor Swift

PROLOGUE: BEFORE THE ALBUM DROPS

Overbearing yet meticulous, Maura had successfully prevented even a drop of paint from spilling onto any unwanted surface in the apartment. Even though they still had to fold up the tarps, Zachary knew she would be proven right. It was hard to say for Zachary if it would have been better if that were not the case.

The two of them had been at it all day, feeling blessed that this was the last task left before they were officially settled into their new place in Midtown.

They lived on the twelfth floor, providing them with a gorgeous view of Memphis. On top of that, it was the first time in either of their lives that they hadn't lived in a shit-hole. Mostly it had been trailer parks for Maura. Zachary had grown up on a farm in a ramshackle house.

Which was why Zachary thought it was too bad they were going to have to leave it behind so soon. He wasn't going to force the issue— not anymore. Zachary knew she was going to have to reach that conclusion on her own.

That was until an explosion from across the street poised Maura to tackle Zachary onto the ground. Maura threw a roller in her hand (dabbed in the pale yellow paint she had chosen in hopes of visual serenity), and it landed on the ground before they did.

They remained there as the explosion subsided, astonished to be alive. Zachary knew it was time to get the old argument going again. He was hesitant to do so, but it was becoming a matter of life and death. Gripping her left shoulder, he said, "I have our bags packed and ready. We need to go."

"No." She bolted up from the floor, going to turn on the television.

"Maura, we should at least leave until we know what that was."

"It was another helicopter crash," she said, looking at the television.

"It's not safe. Look, you got paint on the floor," Zachary said, pointing to the skewed yellow spill near the roller.

"If the news tells us to evacuate, we will."

A plume of smoke hit their window, bouncing and trailing off in every direction outside until it finally began to seep inside.

Zachary hated that damn television she'd bought for the apartment. But Maura needed to watch her Tampa Bay Rays every season. To him, television drove people apart while trying to sell them shit from that disconnection. Worst of all, it would not tell them to evacuate.

A whimpering Barney came out from the bedroom, his nap disturbed. The pudgy Beagador fled to a detached Maura. Zachary paid no attention to what the news was saying. Maura seemed to know this and was calling the details out to him while he tried to get the paint off the floor, hoping to clean off any trace before it dried.

"Traffic copter. No one will say from which station. Hmm. Could be this one. This is going to get interesting."

The cold reality of his relationship with Maura was that she called the shots, and he had to deal with it. But not this time. He'd had enough. Too many times he'd been too worried about losing her to get nasty in their arguments. Instead, he'd sufficed to let her have her way. While he walked into the living room, something fell from the top of the building across the street to the ground below. Whatever it was was on fire, and an overwhelming stench perpetrated through the window and into their nostrils. Zachary overestimated his bravery as he sat in front of the television.

Maura looked taken aback.

"Why, Maura? The world is fucking ending all around us, and you want to act like everything is normal!"

"Okay, dear." The television was still on behind her. It was a commercial. "First of all, I got the scholarship. Second off, look, our place is ready. It's livable and all!"

"Do you realize what's happening out there right now?" he asked her.

"I got the scholarship." Her grip on Barney tensed for a moment, then she relaxed.

"It's not safe to be watching that anymore." Zachary gestured to the television, knowing eventually, the report would come in about what the helicopter pilot had been doing. It had to be the new song that had hit the airwaves, of that he had no doubt. Thank God he hadn't heard it yet. Apparently, it was actually called "I'm Not Brainwashing You." It was only a matter of time before it showed up in some car commercial. Or they announced the date the whole album would be released.

"Zach, we have nowhere to go."

"I get that, hun. But you're savvy. We have to make due. One day, the album's going to drop, and it'll be too late." Why was he talking about the album? It freaked him out because he feared the stories had to be true. It was practically all anyone talked about these days.

"I got the scholarship," she repeated, now walking around behind the couch, her fingers tensing into fists then releasing.

"You really did. And I'm so proud of you. But that's not going to matter to people so much these days."

"I spend years working myself out of nothing. I did four fucking years in the army for them to rule every aspect of my life. What? For nothing?"

"Not for nothing." Zachary did his best to reassure her, closing in on her while she paced back and forth. "We can protect ourselves and care for each other out there. This whole thing could blow over, and we could be back here in no time." He wished he hadn't said that, but it was all right. She surrendered.

Once he calmed her down, they grabbed their bags. Barney followed after them. Zachary realized the packs he'd prepared would be too heavy for the distance they were going to have to travel.

"One more thing before we go," said Maura.

"What's that?"

"Well, we're not coming back. We're in agreement, right?"

"What?"

"Zachary, don't be daft. This isn't going to just blow over like some breaking news story." She went back into the living room and smashed the mounted LCD against the wall. "There, happy? Only for you, baby."

"I would have liked to have done that," said Zachary.

Maura smirked. It remained until they entered the panic of the city block below.

Trying to stay in one spot proved to be nearly impossible. If they found a place that was safe and isolated, they soon ran out of food and were forced to go searching. Most groceries stores and gas stations were rapidly no longer being tended to and fell to looters and disrepair. Maura left her pistol, a Smith & Wesson, protruding out of her left pocket in its black leather holster at all times.

The plan was to move as far away from Tennessee as possible. The center of the madness was taking place in Nashville. Zachary wanted to go south, believing the Central American population wouldn't be as affected as less of them understood English. They were forced to turn back after they heard that wasn't the case. The justification Maura had given him was something he simply didn't fight and couldn't even remember amongst all the other burdens of being nomadic survivors in a crumbling society. Maybe something to do with proximity.

All towns and cities were warzones. The album had dropped, and its spread made it too risky. They believed it wouldn't be long before they were found and were forced to listen to it too. It was now just a matter of having another day together where they could be human— that's all they could ask for.

Barney was long gone, separated from them during an attack. Animals were immune to the affliction, as far as they could tell, but who knew what the future would hold. Would some singing bird chirp the ongoing insanity into their ears?

They spent their nights in a worn-off green tent. Once, the two of them set-up for a night and stayed in a forest clearing off a highway for over two weeks, tired of the aches compounded by the walking. Dire thirst overtook them, and they were forced to boil water from a stream. Though this frightened them enough to be on the move again, bottled water became more and more a scarcity the more stores they dared to stop in.

Zachary stumbled across the road with Maura leading them to a garden shop with a greenhouse. His stamina left much to be desired.

"It's beautiful," said Maura, looking to the greenhouse then up at the sky.

"Not so fast," Zachary told her. They approached slowly until they realized most of the items on display hadn't been watered for some time. As a result, they were either rotting or dead. "Well, it seems fine actually. Let's find some water and move on."

"Why don't we hang out here?" Maura suggested. "Stay indoors for once. I bet the hose still works."

"I guess, Maura. There's no guarantee this place is abandoned. Wish we could check that radio." It sat on the windowsill of the front porch. There was no use risking it. It was exactly how those songs had gotten everyone.

"When's the last time we came into contact with

anyone?" she asked him. That logic was not very satisfactory to him, but he knew she needed some rest.

Inside they found a cooler below the cash register filled with soda cans and bottled water. Zachary grabbed two water bottles, and they sat down against the wall. Curled up next to each other, they dosed off in a cozy position. Although it was getting colder outside due to an approaching winter, the collected heat from the sunlight in the shop made them lazy.

For a little over an hour, they got their rest, but in a failing world such as this, it wasn't long before they were at the wrong end of a gun.

"Hey, get up!" said a voice.

Maura and Zachary opened their eyes. Two men stood over them, both toting shotguns. Zachary saw Maura go for her gun. It was hardly subtle.

"Wrong fucking place to go to sleep, folks," said the man on the left. He was heavyset with long curly hair that needed to be cut. The man on the right didn't have anything to say. His face was gaunt and held a detached look with an even scrappier head of hair.

"Why do you say that?" asked Zachary casually. He dreaded Maura's instinctual response to these dangerous situations. As the seconds inched by, her hands stayed frozen and visible on her sides. Most nights, she'd sleep with her gun closer to her than she kept him.

"People more adaptable than you could take liberties," said the heavyset man.

"Though this isn't the best way to introduce ourselves, may I suggest you leave us be?" Zachary requested. "We're not infected, and I think our kind is growing more and more valuable each day."

"What, the stupid assholes who nod off in the middle of the day, just begging to be sacked?"

"Yeah, whatever, asshole," said Maura.

"Sassy bitch, eh, Evan?" He turned to the man on the

right. "It's been awhile for you, hasn't it?"

Evan shook his head. "Fuck this. Leave that chick alone, Trevor. I don't feel good. It's coming on."

"Not now!"

Evan dropped his shotgun and slowly sat down across from where Maura and Zachary were. The heavyset man was yelling at Evan while still pointing his shotgun at Maura and Zachary.

Confused, Zachary asked, "Are we done here?"

The heavyset man growled at Zachary, then crouched down to Evan's side.

Just then, they heard the sound of cars coming their way.

"Someone's in a hurry," said Maura. "You're not alone, are you?"

"It's just the two of us," Evan mumbled.

"Let's hope they're nicer than you," said Zachary. He nudged Maura to indicate they should turn the tables on Evan and the other man, perhaps take them out before the couple found themselves threatened again.

The two cars engines grew louder and louder between gunshots being fired.

"Fuck, not now!" The heavyset man said. Evan had collapsed onto the floor. He slapped Evan's cheeks. "Wake up, man."

"What's happening?" asked Zachary, pushing himself up.

"I don't know whose coming but—"

The car whipped into view and turned directly to the greenhouse, inevitably smashing through it.

"Help me move him. He's important!" demanded the heavyset man. His attention was completely focused on the unconscious Evan.

Maura and Zachary took their chance. "Not to us," said Maura. They picked the shotguns up and threw them behind the counter. Maura took out her pistol.

"Fine, be like that. Kill us now or help us out! But I believe he's immune."

The other car skidded to a stop just outside the shop. After the three of them had finished dragging Evan behind the counter, Maura and Zachary took possession of the shotguns and kept them aimed at the two men.

"If they start playing music, hum your favorite song to yourself," said the heavyset man. "Focus hard as hell on it. That's what he told me to do. How to reduce your chances of turning."

"Wasn't that your problem with us?" asked Zachary. "Sleeping at the wrong time?"

Maura was about to tell Zachary to shut the hell up, but the explosion did that for her. Evan was roused. The second vehicle was destroyed, along with whoever or whatever had been inside of it.

There was no activity for some time. The four of them waited then went together to see what had happened outside. Still aiming at Evan and his companion, Maura and Zachary went over to the greenhouse ready for more shooting.

A blue SUV was on its side, having displaced glass, pottery, and plants upon its collision. That's when they noticed him.

An old man was smoking a cigarette against the underside of the upturned car. The crash had left him bruised and bleeding, but still on his feet. His beard was short and trimmed. The prominent feature of a missing left earlobe drew everyone's attention, an old scar.

In his arms was a young brunette-haired girl with a ponytail. He waved to them with his left arm and gestured down a rifle he'd dropped next to the tire.

"Hi, I'm Liam. They're still able to drive, it seems."

"So you're not one of them?" asked Maura, already assured of the answer.

"No, I prefer classic rock. Although, when it's considered *classic* is a discussion that's liable to piss me off." He turned to head to the car burning away on the road. "They wanted us both for the fan club, but we weren't interested. Tried to pick them all off for amusement, but it's like they hum those lyrics and can't feel pain."

The man looked remarkably familiar to Maura. She'd seen his face somewhere. Her memory was good. But after scouring her mind, she came up empty. It would come to her. "Who's the girl?"

"I'll tell you later, over dinner if you want some bread. Freshly baked this morning. See that out there?" He pointed back to the wreckage beyond the greenhouse. "It's why I need to accept bread is too much of a luxury these days. There's plenty to spare for now, though."

"We'll pass," said Zachary. "I mean, these guys just tried to do us in."

"Tables turned somehow, huh? Sure. Let's talk this out, all. I think we should stick together. This youngin could use some better company than me." He lifted her up a little. Besides a bit of blood trailing down from her forehead, she looked uninjured. "She's okay. Just a little woozy. So you're not getting along so well?"

"These guys were about to kill us," said Maura.

"Nuh-uh!" protested the heavyset man.

"Or something," said Zachary.

"Before we settle this, Liam, are there any more coming?" asked Evan.

"Always," said Liam.

PART
ONE

"Hey, monkey see, and monkey do
Must I get brainwashed by what's surrounding you?
Didn't you know that every little thing's contagious
Oh, yes, every little thing's contagious"
-Skye Sweetnam

ONE

Looking over a large puddle that had formed from an overflow of the river, Leigh's shoulders were hunched forward the way her mother would chastise her about. Eying the movement of the water back and forth, it made her realize what was next. She knew it as a certainty that, as Maura had put it, anything could happen.

Given the attitude of the others, it seemed natural. They were acting excited to go down again, and she didn't understand it. Hadn't they settled into their new lives? Survived another winter intact? Their intentions, because they were noble, were something Leigh was afraid to speak out against. But if just one of them felt the same way as she did, besides Evan that is, maybe she could convince them to call the whole thing off. Evan hadn't asked for this, that's what got her. It was all Trevor's idea. That fat ass-aholic fuck, as Leigh had heard Maura address him. With Evan getting progressively worse, the others had just grown weary of Trevor's protestations to staying put.

"I wouldn't object to euthanasia," Evan had told them a few weeks ago. "It's going to kill me this time, guys."

"Yeah, maybe, Evan," said Trevor, who had been standing above him to stave off the sunlight. Evan loved the sun, but it was not good for him anymore. "But what if it's just a flare-up? You never found out enough to say something like that for sure."

"Does it matter? I could be dying. It's probably worth betting on."

"Fuck yeah, it matters," Trevor countered, patting Evan on the head. "Boy, we just gotta get you some help. Some meds. What you had before."

"There's none of that out here," said Evan. "And we *can't* go back. These mountains have kept us safe and you all know it's still bad down there."

That should have been it. But some more time passed, and now they were about to risk all of their lives for Evan.

"Leigh," Mr. Bennett called out from faraway. His voice was stern, urgent. It was against their rules to move this far out from the established boundary alone, but to Leigh, it seemed like they enforced the rules much more with her. She waited a few seconds longer and dabbed her fingers in the frigid, slushy water.

"Here," she shouted back to him.

"Well, come on back, Leigh," he said. "Time to eat." The end of his sentence trailed away as he walked back. Leigh moved the branches and shrubbery aside to reach the makeshift path to the elevated clearing. That's where the six of them hid from the world, trying to survive as long as they could. The only amenity left besides some rationed preservatives was toilet paper. It was supposed to be where they stayed. But with Evan's illness ramping up, they would be on the move again soon.

Running to catch up to Mr. Bennett, Leigh watched as he turned around to face her. He nodded in disapproval. "Don't do that, Leigh."

"I think you'd hear them coming, Mr. Bennett," she said, speeding past the old man before he was finished looking her over.

"Yes, I suppose you'd be singing by now too." They reached the campsite where the fire Leigh had started all by herself crackled along with the sound of boiling water. Evan tended to it on his own, giving Leigh pangs of guilt. It was supposed to be on her to prepare dinner that night, and she'd blown it off.

"Where's Trevor?" Leigh asked Mr. Bennett, seeing Maura and Zachary were inside their tent.

"Busy, I imagine. Leigh, help Evan out. Jesus."

"Okay, okay, I'm sorry." She hadn't realized her irresponsibility would lead to Evan struggling.

"It's okay, Leigh. I mean I've been so useless lately. It's good to focus on something simple."

"Shush. I've got this." She took over stirring the rice in the pot suspended over the fire by the carefully arranged sticks. Evan went to feed more wood into the fire, but Leigh stopped him and did it herself.

"Rest, Evan!"

"All right, all right."

A few minutes later, Trevor was back and sat down by the fire.

Mr. Bennett joined shortly after. "Look, Leigh, before we set out in a few days, I thought I should go over any questions you might have." The guy just couldn't shake his old teaching habits. She supposed it didn't help that she had to call him Mr. Bennett. The days were filled with verbal quiz questions, like her education still meant anything these days. She was glad she never had him as a real teacher.

"No. Unless there's any new information that was discussed while I was off—"

"Yeah, off where, Leigh?" Trevor cut in.

"Don't even start," cautioned Leigh, knowing she had no right to speak so curtly to him but not caring.

Trevor's finger shot up and pointed to Mr. Bennett, scooping some rice into his bowl. "He went out of his way to save your life on that school bus, Leigh. You could be a whiny little shit to me, but at least do something when he asks you. Not only do you abandon your duties, but you also risk exposure going out alone like that."

"I'd say I can't stay holed up here all the time, but it's not a problem now that we're leaving, Trevor," said Leigh.

"She's right. She needs time alone," said Mr. Bennett. "That's why I suggested you take Maura with you, just to keep an eye on you."

"That's not alone!"

"It's as good as you're going to get," said Trevor. "None of us are going off alone once we leave. At all. Maybe when we get back."

"We can stay," said Evan.

"No. We're going to get you some treatment and haul ass back here," said Trevor, looking over to his friend. He looked back at Leigh. "And you are going to follow the rules."

Leigh was by far the youngest, so to her, it was like having five parents all at once. It was awful. "Okay, I'm sorry, but I'm tired of apologizing for everything," said Leigh, squinting her eyes at Trevor. She took the pot off of the fire.

"Fine," said Trevor. "Honesty's the last thing we have, so that's good to know. Anything else you want to say?"

"Can we all just have a quiet dinner for once?" asked Maura, walking over to them. Zachary was behind her, rubbing his eyes.

"Ah, the sleeping lovers poke their heads out for food."

As the notion of a quiet dinner was stomped out through the usual arguments, Leigh stopped listening. Her worries about leaving the mountains ruined her appetite, and she wanted to run away, to make them panic.

Leigh settled for climbing up her favorite tree, which was still in the vicinity of the campsite but high up enough so she couldn't hear them unless they yelled. Climbing up to the highest branch she could, she looked at the stars. The view calmed her, though the wind caused her to shiver.

As a young girl, she could certainly understand why the others were so protective of her. Why their formation for going down from the mountains was to surround her the entire time. It wasn't just a pseudo-parental instinct in them. She was one of the last healthy human girls in the world.

It frightened her to think of how they'd bring it up to her, and when.

Breeding. There had been subliminal hints and indirect, casual talks, but nothing concrete or final had come out of it. All she wanted was a choice in the matter. Just like abortion was a woman's choice before her time. It should be up to her if she wanted to bear children, and under what circumstances. And that was assuming they survived their trial of finding medication for Evan.

What was the point of having a family in a world like this? Children weren't exactly an appealing concept when the world was full of horrible brainless monsters. So why even get into all the messy particulars in the first place? So whoever has sex with her could get off in tandem with feeling like it was for humanity's continued existence?

No way. She wouldn't let any of them near her. Even the burly Zachary, who was cute to her. That was Maura's boyfriend. Let him impregnate her. Leigh hoped when the topic came up, Maura would be on Leigh's side of the argument. One positive thing about Evan's situation was the issue had gone onto the back burner indefinitely. They might all die just because Evan was supposedly immune to the effects of the songs.

Leigh looked above her, and there was the sky, looking no different from when she was just a child, before all this.

"Even Without High Heels"

Written by Taylor Swift

[Verse]
I'm, I'm on the top of a roof
But it's, not that simple
I've, I've got fame, fortune, and fans
Yet pushing things away

With abandon, he walks up to me
At first, I blow him off like my cat does to me
But then I realize my life is a joke
So I admit to cuddling with a boy who is super short

[Chorus]
It's the limit of my dignity
Just so I can push him away you see
Even without high heels
He's so short and thus unsuitable to me

But why did I let him in?

[Verse]
It's been a really long time
I've hurt every boy so out of line
He's all that's left, and I'm going to hate myself
So I escape into my songwriter's playhouse

[Chorus]
It's the limit of my dignity

Just so I can push him away you see
Even without high heels
He's so short and thus unsuitable to me

[Bridge]
Oh, why'd I cuddle with a boy shorter than me?
Even without high heels, he's still shorter than me
I'd love to know when my true will see
I may be Taylor Swift, but I still need attention!

[Chorus]
It's the limit of my dignity
Just so I can push him away you see
Even without high heels
He's so short and thus unsuitable to me

TWO

In her tent, Leigh was woken up by Maura. It was the morning of their departure.

"Things are going to get dicey down there," Maura said.

Leigh reached out and stroked Maura's hair. "So that means I can dye my hair, right?"

"Christ, Leigh. No." Maura pulled away.

"But you get to dye yours?"

"Yes," she said. Maura's hair was purple when she met Leigh, but the months hiding in the mountains had faded it to a blur of white, blonde, and a pale hint of purple. "I'm an adult."

"I'm not even going to get a chance to be an adult, and I want blue hair," Leigh protested as the two of them exited the tent.

"Pipe down," said Trevor. He was focused on the sky, seeing the gray overcast, and groaning.

Evan and Mr. Bennett were overlooking the guns and packing ammo away, the last thing that needed to be done before they could set out.

"We should have done this last night," said Evan.

"You fell asleep. Don't you remember?" said Mr. Bennett sympathetically.

"That's Lupus for you."

"You need a doctor," said Maura.

"Don't ignore me," Leigh said to Maura.

"She's going to be a problem," said Trevor.

Maura walked over to Trevor. "You aren't exactly a solution yourself, Trevor." She walked on as Leigh followed her, repeating her case for why Maura should let her dye her hair. Primarily, because Maura shouldn't have any say in the matter. "Zachary, darling, hurry up!"

"I'm coming, honey." He was nearby in some bushes, using the bathroom. Privacy had been completely evaporated among them after the years went by.

As Leigh went on, Maura had finally had it. She raised her left hand and balled it up. Her wrist snapped due to the rigid, sudden motion. Then her fingers uncurled and curled. She shook her fist over Leigh's head. "Leigh. First off, your parents would say no. I'm sure of it. Second off, I'd have to do your hair because you have never done it before and if you think you can follow the directions on the bottle without fucking up, I'd tell you from experience you're wrong."

"My parents are dead," retorted Leigh.

"So are mine," said Maura. "Probably. Hopefully. What's your point?"

"When am I going to be old enough so you'll let me?"

"It's not a question of age, Leigh. It's about maturity. And not pestering us all the time just because we're trying to protect you. A blue head is a target. Brunette, not quite as much. The swifties dislike that Goth look. It sets them off. It's not really demonstrative of pop or country."

"Yeah? What about purple?"

"I'm wearing a hat."

"So are you coloring your hair again just to spite me?" asked Leigh.

Maura turned a glaze to Leigh, changing an angry expression on Leigh's face into a blank one. "No, you're just a teenage battlefield right now, and it seems like everyone's against you. When, really, you have no idea how far we're willing to go for you."

They returned to Evan and Mr. Bennett. Mr. Bennett distributed their weapons. "Trevor and Maura are the only ones who have any worthwhile experience with a gun, so they get the good stuff." He handed Trevor the AR-19.

Mr. Bennett turned to Maura. "And for you," he handed

her the Winchester. "Stay close to Leigh."

"Why can't I have my own gun?" asked Leigh.

They ignored her. "We should all take turns handling each other's guns, in case we ever have to use them exclusively," reasoned Mr. Bennett. "Ammo goes quick in these firefights."

"Usually, I'd tell you to shove it, but I agree," said Trevor.

"What's everyone so grumpy jamna?" wondered Evan. "Shit, I meant grumpy about… That's not even a word."

"Never mind, Evan. Let's just finish this," said Mr. Bennett.

"Hey, don't cut him off," objected Trevor. "We're all just tired, Evan."

"Ah, me too, man."

"Hang in there, buddy."

Mr. Bennett continued. "Zachary keeps his Glock since he's never used it anyway, and I'll take your Smith & Wesson, Maura. As for you, Evan, hang onto your shotgun."

"Okay," said Evan.

"Don't we have six guns?" asked Leigh.

"Yeah," said Mr. Bennett. "But there's no use carrying the other shotgun. We don't have ammo for it."

"Yep, whatever." She started to prepare breakfast.

She saw Zachary attending to his project of logging their time since the world ended. He'd been lazy in keeping up with it, so much so they weren't sure the date or the year, and only fairly certain of their ages. But they estimated it had been about two years since the album had dropped.

"Not a good sign," Zachary said to Mr. Bennett. There were only two pages left on his memo pads.

"A lot of stuff can fit on four sides," said Mr. Bennett. "Besides, we'll find you some more paper. Probably by the end of the day."

"Yeah, and it's not like anything exciting happened this past week," said Trevor.

"Ah, you've still got it all wrong," said Zachary. "It's not about that. It's about finding something to write about."

"So you don't get bored and say fuck it all, eh, kid?"

Once breakfast was eaten, they all pitched in to break down their setup by the fire pit. Afterward, they were held up by Evan, who tried meditating for twenty minutes while rubbing a rash on his arm before giving up and leading the way to the road. Leigh wished she could just stay behind with Evan and take care of him. It didn't even seem like he was well enough to walk, especially the distance they were in for. And those monstrous fiends that had taken over the world would be on the lookout for humans.

Forty minutes downhill with the burden of her backpack, Leigh announced, "This is a fucking suicide run." She shrugged her shoulders to adjust the straps around her several times in a row.

"That isn't doing you any good," Mr. Bennett said. "The backpack is just coming down on you in the same areas where you're sore."

"We'll take a break soon," said Maura. Leigh could tell she was lying. Maura had exercised every morning before the others were awake, and she probably wasn't feeling the strain yet.

"Leigh's right, guys," said Evan.

"Shut up, Evan," said Trevor.

"Just shoot me."

"We don't have the bullets to spare for that," said Mr. Bennett in a stern voice. He cleared his throat immediately after he had said it. "And if Trevor's story is true, there's a slim chance some scientist could study why you're immune."

"I don't even believe Trevor's story, so who knows?" said Evan. "That could have just been a fluke."

The sun was over them, lighting their way, but barely doing anything to warm them up. The only good thing about the pace they walked was the cold wasn't getting to

Leigh.

Eventually, the path they had deviated from long ago appeared, and they followed the man-made trail all the way down. Getting to I-65 took most of the daylight from the sky.

"At least we're safe around here," said Zachary. The highway was full of long abandoned cars, some crashed into one another. As far as they could tell, it went on for miles in either direction.

"Let's check them out and see if there's anything worth salvaging," said Trevor.

"It's raining," complained Leigh. In reality, Leigh had felt a few light drops come down from the sky. "And what if one of the radios comes on?"

"Relax," said Mr. Bennett in front of her. "Their batteries are long dead. We couldn't get these cars started if we wanted to. See if you can find an umbrella."

"Man, after we get Evan all set, you know where we should go next?" Zachary asked them.

"Where's that?" asked Trevor.

"The sea."

"Again with the ocean," Maura said, sighing.

"Come on, guys. It's the perfect hideaway! We'd have it all to ourselves. We'd just have to veer towards the Carolinas and find a ship."

"It would take a long time to get there," said Mr. Bennett. "I love the idea of the ocean. I think it's safer than the mountains, but one plan before the other, Zachary."

"It'd be lovely, hun, but Liam's right," said Maura.

"I take it I don't have a say," said Leigh. "I did get seasick once, you know."

"It's nothing to worry about right now, Leigh," said Maura. She looked down the highway and saw a road sign. "No fucking way." She began walking to it quickly, although it was at least a mile away. No one followed her.

"Oh, fine. Let her go off alone," said Leigh.

"I'm going to find some goodies," said Trevor. "Let's meet back here in fifteen or something. Evan, take a break, man. You're killing me."

"Sure thing, Trevor."

Zachary, Mr. Bennett, and Leigh followed Maura to the right side of the shoulder to see the sign, which had originally been an indicator for a gas station and a McDonald's 0.4 miles further down the road. Now it read TAYLOR SWIFT OR DIE in dried blood. The rain had washed some of the streaks away, but the sentence was unmistakable.

"See, this is the sort of thing you'd never see in the middle of the ocean," said Zachary.

"This means they've got to be nearby," said Maura, biting her lip. She frequently turned to her left and right after she saw the sign.

"They don't just walk around congested highways like this," said Mr. Bennett. "It's abnormal."

"I think we should just get what we can from the cars and find a place to crash for the night," said Zachary.

"Fine with me," said Leigh. She walked over to a sedan and disengaged the trunk latch from under the driver's seat. A dead body was reclined in the passenger seat. The stink was enough to bring tears to Leigh's eyes. There was a gunshot wound in the body's neck and dried blood on the inner side of the door. It was a teenage boy a little bit older than her. She wondered for a moment if he had been cute. It was hard to tell. The smell of dead bodies no longer made Leigh sick. Regardless, she left the boy to check the trunk, which Zachary was already rifling through.

"Nice, more road flares," said Zachary. "Tire iron?" He offered the metal cross-bar to Leigh.

"I'll have to pass. I can change a tire without such sophisticated technologies."

"Psssh." Out of everyone, Leigh liked Zachary the best. He hardly ever criticized her when she didn't meet the group's expectations of her. And on top of that, he treated

Maura like a queen. "You know, Leigh, I know it sounds insane, but I hope you think about the ocean. No one takes me seriously, but I really want it to happen. We could find more people on the way, maybe ditch Trevor and Evan once we've helped them out, you know?"

"That'd be nice. I think. I never thought of it. Like I said, though, I got seasick once when I was a kid."

"Be ready to give it another chance. You never know. We could sail off anywhere in the world. Why I bet some parts of the world are still totally off-the-grid and unaffected by what happened. Villages and everything. So far out from the cities that we'd never have to worry."

"That does sound nice. Why don't we just go for it now?" asked Leigh.

"Trevor might be a dick, but Evan's too awesome to leave to the wolves. You know?"

"I guess."

After checking a few more cars, they heard screaming then two gunshots. They regrouped with Maura and Mr. Bennett. Running to the source of the commotion, they saw Evan walking over to them. "It was Trevor."

"Do we have company?" Mr. Bennett asked urgently.

"No. He was screaming because… I don't know. Something spilled on him and ate right through him. He was suffering so I shot him."

"What?!" asked Maura. "Is he dead?"

"Yes," said Evan. "He was suffering, Maura. I panicked."

They went to check Trevor's body out, and sure enough, Mr. Bennett identified chemical burns from Trevor's clothes and the lower half of his body. It wasn't hard to tell, even from where Leigh stood away from the truck he'd been checking out. "He wouldn't have made it. You did the right thing, Evan."

"It smells like rotten eggs and boogers," said Zachary. There was a massive cylinder container that had spilled and whatever was inside of it had also eaten away at the backseat of the truck and even some decay below that.

"Some kind of acid. Sulfuric? Possibly fluoroantimonate? What the hell. In a car, though?"

"He was opening the truck-bed, and that shit just got all over him," explained Evan. "From that drum there. Must have been rigged like a trap. He was fine for a few seconds, but the smell got to him. He wanted to rinse off with more than the rain and— it activated."

We've got to get out of here," said Mr. Bennett. "This was a freak accident, but those gunshots will attract attention. Some savvy citizen was probably carting it around in his car as a weapon. Evan, did he or any of it touch you?"

"No. He kept running away from me when I tried to get close."

"Jesus," said Maura.

"You didn't see anyone, did you?" asked Zachary to Evan.

"No. But we're out in the open. This is just going to keep happening until we're all gone." Evan looked over Trevor. "He took care of me way too well."

They saw strange squirt guns in the truck but decided not to take them, because Mr. Bennett said whatever chemical it was would be too dangerous to play with.

Sleep did not come easy for them that night, but no swifties came for them.

The subject of turning back was not broached, and Leigh realized that if it had been Evan who'd died instead of Trevor, that's exactly what they'd be doing.

THREE

On their fourth day out from the mountains, Leigh and the others spotted some swifties. They were loud, obnoxious, and thus made their presence known from a distance. Leigh and the others approached with extreme caution from the woods along the highway.

Maura counted six of them, probably armed. They danced slowly around a car that was on fire while an eighteen-wheeler with a large plow attached to it was smashing into all the abandoned vehicles, sloppily knocking them into the shoulder. It had been the group's hope that the swifties would not still be mentally capable of driving. But apparently, they could.

"No doubt that truck is blasting Taylor. Close-range combat is out of the question," said Zachary. They had ear protection, but there was no telling how well it would work against the music's effects. Little was known to them about how it changed a person into a swiftie. One thing they did know was it didn't take much, because most of the world had been turned, largely from inadvertently listening to the radio or watching television.

"They can't ride the truck into the woods if we get close enough to snipe them out," said Maura.

"Not even you are that good of a shot," said Mr. Bennett. Leigh saw his face grimace. "How do these assholes still know how to drive?"

"Do you think they have a communication system? To alert others?" asked Evan, who was surprisingly alert that day.

"Maybe they have walkie-talkies," said Mr. Bennett. "C/B? Nothing fancier than that."

They assessed their options, knowing their opposition was getting closer and closer to them.

"We're running out of time. We need to figure out something," Leigh said. Mr. Bennett had reluctantly allowed Leigh to carry the Smith & Wesson, while he had allocated the AR-19 to Maura and taken his Winchester back from her. Leigh needed Maura's permission to use it, but she felt good to be armed, even though shooting left her uncontrollably shaky.

They considered going around the swifties or letting them pass. But then the music would be in their hearing range until they retreated. Evan's hypothesis as to his immunity to the effects of the Taylor Swift music had something to do with altered focus. He'd been trying to teach them how he accomplished that by use of a little toy xylophone. The logic was that if they focused on one melody well enough while the Taylor Swift songs were being heard, it prevented the damaging effect listening to Taylor Swift's music had.

The problem was that the little xylophone and the theory hadn't been proven. Evan only had one experience that he'd narrowly avoided with Trevor's help.

"On top of that, we're just going to run into more swifties avoiding these," said Zachary.

"We need something we can drive anyway," said Evan. "That truck seems like serendipity to me."

"If only there was a way to take out the drive, bum-rush our way inside, and shut off the music. Then we could mow them down," said Leigh, gesturing to the brainwashed fans.

"They're probably just going to work a little while longer and head back," said Mr. Bennett. "This is an opportunity we can't pass up."

Zachary looked anxiously over from Mr. Bennett to Maura, knowing they would make the decision.

"Why don't we just go for it?" asked Maura.

"No plan?" asked Leigh.

"No… okay, wait. I'll fire two shots back-to-back in

their direction. It'll draw their attention to me. When they're fixing in on me, Zachary, Liam, and Evan, you get behind them and hit them as hard and as fast as you can."

"Before we get anywhere near that truck, we need to make sure... yeah," said Mr. Bennett. There was no music coming from the truck, but the swifties were reciting lyrics in monotone, something about burning a picture.

As they executed the plan, both of Maura's shots missed the ones she'd targeted. Leigh watched it all, waiting for a chance to shoot at a swiftie. Instead of going in Maura's direction, the six swifties fled into the semi-trailer of the truck, forcing Zachary, Mr. Bennett, and Evan to stay hidden. They wanted to ambush the swifties where they were hiding, but the truck began driving away.

Maura managed to take out the driver, sending the truck back into the cars the driver had placed on the shoulder of the road.

A few of the swifties made for the front cab to get control of the truck. Mr. Bennett and Zachary were screaming out the lyrics to Bruce Springsteen's "Dancing In The Dark" in anticipation of the truck's music turning on.

"Come on," said Maura to Leigh. "This is our only chance."

Leigh didn't argue. While they made their way to the truck, Maura did the best she could to keep the AR-19 she held fixed on the rear cab. Maura saw someone's head poke out, and she let off a round of bullets, steadying the assault rifle after each shot. The men had finished with disposing of the driver, an elderly black man whose blood was all over the seat. Mr. Bennett took the wheel. Maura raced over to the truck and got in, sitting on Zachary's lap. The space was so tight that Leigh had to sit on Evan's lap.

The engine was still on, so Mr. Bennett floored the accelerator. Some of the swifties jumped out of the back and started firing at them. Maura wanted to go in reverse to run them over, but Mr. Bennett resolved that it would be too difficult to turn, and by the time they did, the swifties would have taken out the tires.

"There could be more swifties in the back waiting for us to stop," argued Maura.

"There's nothing we can do now," said Mr. Bennett. "Let's just get off the highway and hope the road is cleared."

"Then what?" asked Leigh.

"Hope to spot something, anything that can help Evan. A hospital, more survivors."

Before they parked the truck at the gas station, Mr. Bennett once again crashed the truck into a car to rattle any possible stowaways behind them. He did this without warning, side-swiping the much smaller red hatchback parallel parked against the curb.

"What the hell, man?" Maura shouted. "You could have said brace yourself or something. We're not even buckled in."

"And I'm sore," said Leigh.

"Everyone's fine. It wasn't that big of a deal. Can we take care of the semi-trailer, please?" asked Evan.

Mr. Bennett was already on it. Once he had come to a complete stop, he grabbed his Winchester, and the others got out of the truck, Leigh holding the xylophone. It was a one-octave bell set, and all she knew was the first dozen or so notes to "Fur Elise" so she played them over and over again in a loop while walking after Evan, Maura, Zachary, and Mr. Bennett, who was up front. They reached the edge of the semi-trailer, leaning up against it waiting to see if any swifties would come out. Night had come, and they could not see if there were still swifties in there or not. The rear doors were open.

They waited as long as they felt they could for any signs of life, but they couldn't stay in one spot for long. From what they'd seen, the swifties had all left the smaller towns surrounding Nashville in favor of Nashville itself, as that was rumored to be where she had settled to rule from. Regardless, the number of swifties in the world promised that it wouldn't be long before trouble came their way again. Maura and Evan rushed to try to siphon gas while Mr. Bennett and Zachary stayed to wait for any activity. It was best to try to keep and maintain the truck as long as they could, knowing what a hassle it could be to find other vehicles.

They ran their flashlights into the semi-trailer, and Leigh kept playing those same few notes over and over again. Other than that, silence.

"Come out, folks. End of the line!" Mr. Bennett called. He fired a shot from his Winchester, hoping to elicit a response. "Understand?" Swifties were once human. They had a limited understanding of language. A swiftie would be able to respond, they just wouldn't be able to do so in a conventional manner. The last time the group was up against swifties, the swifties spoke entirely in Taylor Swift lyrics.

"Screw that," said Zachary. His impatience compelled him to shoot the AR-19 into the semi-trailer. Leigh watched the shells fall to the ground.

Mr. Bennett immediately chastised Zachary, which made him stop. "Idiot!"

"Sorry. Maura says I need to be less timid." Satisfied, Zachary motioned his flashlight into the semi-trailer. It was full of boxes and green tarps. He leaned in without entering and hands snatched his head and shoulders and pulled him in.

"NO!" said Mr. Bennett, leaping forward after Zachary.

"Help me! Fuck!" Zachary yelled from the dark.

Leigh's tempo slowed down on her partial rendition of "Fur Elise."

Mr. Bennett jumped into the semi-trailer.

Leigh didn't look into the darkness. She simply kept playing. Maura and Evan ran past her and into the semi-trailer after them. The tarps were being tossed aside. There were awful grunting sounds and the swifties were chanting.

Music came on, but it sounded like it was coming from headphones. It had to be Taylor Swift playing. Zachary screamed. The swifties were hurting him.

"Keep playing, Leigh," she heard Evan shout. But Leigh couldn't move. In the span of a few seconds, she was lost. She couldn't help Zachary.

Someone was shooting one of the pistols. It lit up the semi-trailer for milliseconds. Leigh's ears were filled with a piercing drone, a ringing she hadn't had to contend with for months. Luckily, her ear protection was in, muffling the sounds.

One good thing was as her hearing adjusted to the silence, she knew it was over. Leigh watched as the others walked out. Maura, Mr. Bennett, and Evan exited, carrying Zachary. Maura snapped her fingers as Zachary seemed out of it.

"Hey, come back," she demanded.

All Leigh could do was resume "Fur Elise" on the xylophone, although it seemed like the others had managed to destroy whatever music device the dead swifties had.

Zachary was a maddening sight the others tried to calm down. He told them frantically, "They got me, they fucking got me," Zachary said. "They made me listen while they held me down. I'm gone, kill me!"

FOUR

Two of the dead swifties were huge men who looked like bikers, toting leather jackets, and beards. The third one was a little girl, younger than Leigh. Somehow, all three of them had been changed, turned into brainless servants of Taylor Swift.

"They seem to possess more animalistic tendencies than human ones," said Mr. Bennett, "yet, at the same time, they have found a way to communicate amongst themselves to better follow any orders handed down from Taylor herself."

"How did they outsmart Zachary then?" Maura asked. "This should not have happened! The hell is going on, Liam?" As soon as the swifties were confirmed dead, Maura had jumped on them and started punching them, clawing at them. The little girl's eyes were torn out before Mr. Bennett and Evan were able to pull Maura away.

"He was careless."

"He didn't belong in a world like this. He was too sweet. And I egged him on to handle his business."

Leigh was shocked that Maura spoke of Zachary in the past tense like that. She knew what had to be done, but Zachary was still alive. After the music had gone on in the semi-trailer, any of them could have been exposed. But it was Zachary they got, presumably holding him down and making him listen to the device that played back the Taylor Swift album.

Leigh looked over to Zachary. He was bloody and humming whatever song it was the swifties had forced him to listen to. Humming or singing Taylor Swift alone couldn't change someone. It was something found only in Swift's recordings. However, if someone was humming, it was a symptom that they were turning into a swiftie.

Maura was looking down at Zachary, restrained and unresponsive. Listening to what he was humming, she said, "It's goddamn "Teardrops On My Guitar." Fuckers."

Evan had found a pistol on one of the biker swifties. There were only three bullets in the chamber. Not nearly as many as they had used since leaving the mountains.

"We need to move on, Maura," said Mr. Bennett. "Evan and I are going to gas up the truck, and we're leaving this behind. Take care of him fast."

"Yeah," said Maura.

Leigh raced after Mr. Bennett. She pushed him. "Why are you making her do it?!"

Mr. Bennett ignored her.

"Leigh, shhh," said Evan, leaning over to her. "She asked to be the one to do it."

She was too upset to listen to Evan. Going back to Maura, she found Maura crying over Zachary, who simply continued humming and shifting his head from left to right. It wouldn't be long before the humming advanced into singing and anticipation to follow anything Taylor Swift commanded of him. He'd kill Maura without hesitation. It'd been so long since Leigh had lost someone. Not since her family, from before the world had ended. What Leigh remembered most were her parents, school, and music. She never heard music anymore.

The five of them reached an old shack a few hours later, hoping to meet once more with an eccentric old man named Awl. Upon a close inspection of the surrounding area, they decided he was no longer there. A few years ago, while passing through in search of a safe place, they'd met him. The recluse was not interested in joining them, only in bartering.

They decided to take shelter for the night in Awl's shack, knowing Zachary would have to be put down at some point.

It made Leigh remember the lit lanterns that painted the old walls of the shack when Awl told them what he knew about how all this had happened. The tale resonated with her as she prepared to say goodbye to Zachary.

"Taylor Swift was born on December 13th, 1989 in Pennsylvania," Awl began. "Her grandmother, an opera singer, had nurtured her and opened her mind to the idea of performing and writing music. Eventually, Taylor got a guitar and learned to sing. She had substantial support from her family. They actually moved down to Nashville, Tennessee, where Taylor recorded demos and performed wherever she could.

"Something clicked with the powers that be and, at sixteen, Taylor Swift was signed to a major label. That was about 2005. Her debut album quickly found an audience. It was country music. The modern kind, I guess you could say.

"More years passed and the girl gradually transitioned from country into pop, getting a ton of awards in the process and thus becoming a household name. Her target audience was girls just like Leigh. The music was catchy, and the songs were brimming with youth, sometimes reading like a teenager's diary entry.

"Rapper Kanye West humiliated her at the 2009 MTV Music Video Awards, earning him all sorts of flack and creating a pop culture disaster to be discussed for years to come.

"Her influence and fanbase only increased album after album. Taylor was on a roll, becoming one of highest paid performers of the time. With her album *1989*, she once again grew exponentially while fully embracing pop star status. Following a world tour in 2015, she relaxed for a few years. The world at the time was a mess independent of Taylor Swift, but things were still functional. What we call those who've been altered by her, swifties, that was the term that just meant you were a die-hard fan of Taylor Swift.

Even back then, she had a very special relationship with them. Taylor would send Christmas care packages. She once attended a fan's bridal shower, and would also bake them cookies, among other things. Now, like I said, the world was functional, but those swifties became uneasy, they were eager to hear more and not very understanding of the lack of new music from Taylor for another four years.

"When the first new single she released in years did come out, the lyrics boiled down to cuddling with a boy who was shorter than her. The media had a field day, bashing her for being almost thirty and producing such shallow songs. The negative press almost ate her alive. First, she held the release of her next album, then she threatened to give up on music altogether.

"This brings us to the uncertain portion of how this all happened. We remember the swifties and their backlash, becoming extremely militant over Taylor's decision. They didn't blame her, but the critics who attacked her. That's when things really escalated. The sloping bridge from rational human being into how we now define a swiftie. Because if the swifties heard someone talking bad about Taylor Swift or her new song, they would attack them. There were riots and strikes. But the swifties were also increasing in number yet again. No one realized the leaked music from the album was changing people. By the time they did, it was too late. The world fell into chaos as the swifties overtook the human population, even invading Kanye West's home and viciously murdering him. They say he was flayed. It seemed as if it was a zombie invasion, but the Kanye West thing was happenstance. Nonetheless, that's how the world turned. The swifties were united and led by Taylor herself, ushering in a new world order once there were so few of us left. And the album was released and played everywhere, as it and only it can change someone into a swiftie. Something about how catchy the songs were. They get into your head, and you can't get them out. Then there's heavy state of suggestibility as you start blindly following whatever Taylor Swift says. Plenty of conspiracy theory too, because I think Taylor held listening parties and world domination meetings with her fans at her concerts in secret at first. Then the album was even able to brainwash those most critical of Taylor Swift. Just listening to some songs in the background on your way to work could be sufficient. Then you lived a violent, irrational existence as a swiftie with no hope of regaining your humanity.

"Most of the world's turned now and Taylor Swift, as you know, became the queen of the planet, now known as Taylearth. This being at the expense of society. The capital of her kingdom became Nashville, and probably still is. Taylor's wishes were to take over the reins in order to make the world a better place. For that to be done, it required her to hold absolute authority in conjunction with comprehensive mind control. But the vision seems to have become somewhat skewed, since there are still a few humans in the picture, resisting, surviving. Taylor's first major operation as leader was to call for fewer men in the world. A sort of male genocide, a menocide if you will, took place. Now the world's females greatly outnumber the world's males, swiftie or not.

"I myself am getting old and years have gone by. We'll be taken out one by one. If it isn't the roving gangs of swifties or the cold, it'll be the years. Humanity will be bred entirely out of existence, one by one, and the swifties will have things to themselves. I can only hope I don't live to see the day Taylor dies. Anyhow, that's all I know…"

Where was Awl, Leigh wondered. Had the swifties gotten to him? He'd been right. One by one.

Mr. Bennett put Zachary down when Maura faltered.

Zachary was in a daze, having no idea what was happening. Even as Mr. Bennett brandished the Winchester and targeted Zachary's head, Zachary's tenuous grip on his own mind prevented him from knowing he would die.

Swifties were able to communicate with one another through some unintelligible use of Taylor Swift lyrics, but a swiftie in isolation lacked all faculties and nuances swifties in a group possessed, only desiring to listen to more Taylor Swift.

If they waited any longer, Zachary would become a suggestible swiftie, desperate to receive whatever orders Taylor handed down to her denizens.

Since he was already tied to a tree with a rope, Mr. Bennett hesitated no longer. Leigh didn't watch. She closed her eyes and covered her ears. Tears were erupting from her shut eyes as Mr. Bennett pulled the trigger.

Then Zachary was gone, and she did glimpse at the end result. The blood stains on the tree were not as prevalent as Leigh thought they would be. Zachary's head was slumped over, the face disfigured and unrecognizable. Part of her wanted to prepare for her own demise. Awl saying, "One by one," fell into her head as she looked over to his old dwelling place.

There was no doubt in her mind. Leigh finally spoke up about it. "Who's next?" she asked them as Maura prepared Zachary's cremation. To Evan, she said, "I don't want to die!"

"I have something special for you, Leigh," said Mr. Bennett. "I've been saving it a long time." He offered her some chocolate, but she refused.

Maura remained focused on her task, but when it was done, and they were walking off, she went over to Leigh and struck her. Leigh had to take a few steps back and steady herself from falling.

"Zachary sacrificed himself to save you. And Evan. And me. Shut your mouth for once. Nothing is changing right now. Deal with it."

"Why aren't you sad? Why don't you cry?" Leigh asked Maura.

Maura's expression became stern. Leigh turned her gaze to the burning body. Maura's expression did not change as she stared down at Leigh. It seemed as if Maura wanted to smack the girl. Instead, Maura walked away with Zachary's body still on fire behind them. Leigh looked back to him yet again.

PART TWO

"Bad music is a form of murder to the true art of music in general… Bad music has raped an industry that was held up strongly by great expression for decades but now finds itself floundering, giving in to the lowest common denominator of music… Bad music tortures the eardrums and kills little bits of your senses through prolonged exposure… Bad music is a lie, and yet it is foisted on the public in an attempt to turn melodies and songs into hamburgers and fries. Bad music is truly a sin because you don't have to be exceptional to make it in the music industry anymore. You just have to be good enough to stick around and be tolerated."

-Corey Taylor

FIVE

The time since they had left the mountains had seen the deaths of numerous swifties. The semi proved extremely useful, and Mr. Bennett had even mounted speakers onto the truck. He rigged them so while they played Taylor Swift songs, the inside speakers were separate and playing some compact discs they'd found in a department store. The variety of albums led them to wonder about the difference between Taylor Swift's music and others. Exactly what element of sound turned a catchy song into an imperative for doomsday?

"Country music was popular, but only to a certain kind of person," Evan explained to Leigh after showing her some songs from the genre. "Taylor subverted that country music style, which was a kind of niche market, then went on to become a pop star, reaching an even more massive audience."

Leigh found herself drawn to a 90's alternative compilation and played it the most. Track seven came on again, and she asked, "What's this song called?"

"'Semi-Charmed Kind Of Life,'" Maura responded. She was drinking water from a metal container, dented in several places. Leigh wished Maura would express her grief over Zachary. Instead, Maura favored internalization. Leigh's mother would have scolded Leigh for not getting Maura to open up. Then the woman would have also taken a jab at Maura for bottling things up inside.

"It sounds so happy," said Leigh.

"It's a deception then," said Evan. "It's about the abuse of methamphetamines and whatever other drugs you could make out of household ingredients from your local supermarket. The peppy sound is probably supposed to personify being high."

"Good music used to mostly be a result of drugs," said Mr. Bennett. They passed a sign that read they were fifty miles outside of Nashville. It would be foolish to go any closer to any roads leading there. As the hub of Taylor's kingdom, any human would be found and changed. Mr. Bennett turned in a different direction.

"This is what I didn't want, Maura," said Evan.

Maura looked over to him as if she were about to speak. Instead, she lowered her container and crossed her arms.

Leigh used the opportunity to turn up the music.

The results from the speakers were incredible. The swifties they'd drive by would think those in the truck were one of them, then Maura and Evan would shoot them before the swifties knew any better. Maura was insatiable in her kills, wanting to do more than just shoot the swifties as she had done with the ones who turned Zachary. She had eased up on the mayhem after Mr. Bennett censured her, saying it was like torturing individual insects when you had an infestation. He wanted to pass by the swifties since the four of them were getting by unnoticed. Maura was even leaving the bodies out in the open. Leigh made a mental note to listen to Mr. Bennett over Maura from then on, as he had been the voice of reason lately.

Leigh fell in love with the songs from that 90's CD. She happily played it on a loop throughout the days as they inspected empty towns the swifties had abandoned in hopes of finding other survivors or medicine for the feeble Evan. They had managed to find him an anti-malarial at a pharmacy, which he said was close to the stuff he'd taken as treatment for his Lupus before.

Aside from the deaths of Trevor and Zachary, the four of them were feeling optimistic, even discussing driving through to the east coast and going through with Zachary's ocean plans.

There were just so many swifties, and killing them whenever they got the chance eventually to got them into trouble. The Smashing Pumpkins was on one morning when they were trapped by the swifties, who'd set up a road block.

"They're obviously not going to move just because we've got Taylor playing on the outside," said Maura.

"They must be on to us," said Mr. Bennett, accelerating.

"Hold it. What are you doing, Liam?" asked Evan. "Slow down!"

"Your driving has endangered us enough already," said Maura, her voice flat.

"If we *try* to tear through them, we might have a shot at taking them out quickly, finding another car and moving out," said Mr. Bennett.

"Turn around," said Maura.

"Stop," Leigh cried out.

Evan closed his eyes, ostensibly detaching himself from the situation. He was furthest from Mr. Bennett, and Maura's hands slid over the seats, gripping into the remaining scraps of Mr. Bennett's hair and around his missing earlobe, trying to get him to stop.

Leigh wanted to intervene, but she joined Evan in letting the other two have it out.

"Fine, I'm done. I'm not fighting with you, Maura. Just do whatever you want like always. I'm going to get ready to die." He looked over to Evan as Maura switched seats with the old man. "It's not your fault, buddy. There's at least ten swifties, all armed out there. And if they can still operate motor vehicles, I'll bet they sure as hell can still shoot."

Their big rig slowed down, but it was hard to tell if they would make contact with the barrier or not. Already, the swifties were formed at either end of the block and aiming at the truck.

"Yeah, yeah," said Evan, bracing himself. He grabbed onto Leigh. For a moment, Leigh thought of how fragile

Evan was, how strange it was for him to use his malfunctioning body that couldn't even keep itself healthy to protect her. The mind and the body were so separate at times.

"Leigh," said Maura. She turned the wheel to make the truck into a barrier, parallel to the road block a few yards ahead. Leigh reached out her hand, and Maura passed her something. The Glock. "The only reason they haven't fired at us yet, I assume, is because Taylor's playing."

"Reasonable deduction," said Mr. Bennett, looking over the AR-19 and double-checking the ammunition.

"So do we put the plugs in, jump out, and shoot away?" asked Maura.

"There's got to be a point where survival kicks in for them," said Mr. Bennett. "They'll shoot no matter what we're playing."

Leigh stared down at the gun. Maura was a good shot; she'd received a few marksmanship awards in the Marine Corps. Mr. Bennett was all right. Evan might be good for a few shots before something went wrong with him. But her? She certainly had no qualms about killing swifties. They weren't human anymore— they were monsters. The same kind that had destroyed everything she'd knew. The swifties were united under the false guise of Taylor longing for peace. It all sounded so utopian on the surface, but the swifties were mindless animals, barely rational, inundated with pop culture fantasies of escapism. After what Taylor had done with the male population, how could the swifties not realize that? But that was the thing, they could hardly realize anything beyond Taylor. Taylor was their goddess.

"It's now or never, hun," said Maura to Leigh. "We have to do something. And tapping on that xylophone is not going to cut it."

Leigh shoved the Glock back into Maura's hands. "Let me try the rifle, then. And turn that horrible music outside off."

"Nice try, kid," said Maura with an inappropriate smirk, "but you're not going to tinker with the good gun in the middle of a firefight. Move out!"

The four of them piled out of the truck and let off a few shots before the swifties realized they were human. Then Leigh and the others hid behind the truck.

After some quick adjustments and positioning, they were trying to conceal their fear, wanting to get out of the showdown alive.

"Remember, Leigh— accuracy and precision are two different things," said Maura. "And if you don't aim before you shoot, I will hurt you."

"Maura, come on," objected Evan.

"We can't waste any ammo, Evan. I'm with Maura on this one," said Mr. Bennett.

Leigh was on her stomach holding the Glock. Maura was directing her, adjusting her position with her arms.

They were against the rear wheels of the truck. Neither side had fired since the group had found cover. Mr. Bennett kept looking back and forth at the girls and the other end of the road where the swifties hid behind a car.

"You can be afraid, but you need to get control of your shaking," said Maura.

"How do I stop?" Leigh asked her.

"You're giving it a death grip. The harder you hold it, the more it's going to shake."

Leigh tried to loosen her grip, but Maura was dissatisfied. "Too loose!"

"Maybe this isn't the best time to teach her?" Evan suggested.

"What better time than the real thing?" asked Maura.

"Can we focus on taking them out?" asked Mr. Bennett.

"Sure. If we can, we will, Liam. Leigh, take your first shot as soon as one of them pop out."

Leigh aimed. And waited. It seemed like the end of the line to Leigh.

"Now!"

Leigh pulled the trigger of the Glock, and to her surprise, she had the recoil under control. It probably helped that Maura held onto her.

The bullet missed the swiftie.

"Fuck! Get down," Maura said as the stalemate ended and the swifties returned fire.

All the swifties really had to do was put on a Taylor Swift album (every swiftie carried their favorite Taylor Swift album on them at all times) from one of the cars at the roadblock and blast it. The group had ear plugs, but they weren't designed for such eventualities. Fortunately, the swifties favored shooting at them. One of the front tires popped and the truck cab began to lean towards the road.

"It's not like we were going to make it through anyway," said Evan. "Bakkon. I mean..." He trailed off, frustrated. Evan was toting Maura's Smith & Wesson, but he only had about a dozen bullets left.

"Again," Maura said to Leigh. "Try again!" She was pinned against the edge of the truck, cradling the Winchester in her arms. "Enough! We've been here too long." She twisted off her knees into a standing position, then exposed herself. Maura retreated back against the truck as the swifties returned fire again.

"Maybe we could try to trick them into running out of bullets?" wondered Evan.

"Zachary thought he could outsmart them too, Evan," said Maura. "I think they have us this time."

"No suicide runs for you, Maura," said Mr. Bennett.

"Suicide run?" asked Leigh.

"Let me go," said Mr. Bennett. "I'm older."

Leigh held fast to the Glock, aligning the sights and waiting for one of the swifties. She heard what the others were talking about, but it passed through her.

"All they have to do is load a CD, and we're all fucking over," Maura said. "There's four of us and ten of them.

Someone has to go. Me."

"No!" protested Evan. "Let it be me. And you guys retreat. Go back to the mountains or the ocean."

Leigh began singing to herself:

Mary had a little lamb,
Little lamb, little lamb
Mary had a little lamb
Whose fleece was white as snow

It might keep her safe if the swifties decided to end this by pumping their speakers to release the mind-altering sound waves.

They all hesitated to listen to Leigh until she was finished singing. Then more shots came. Maura scooped Leigh up, and they all took cover against the wheel. The shots kept coming, but they no longer seemed to be in their direction. It didn't last long. Then whatever had happened was over. Leigh sang to herself more.

Then they heard shouting. A man's voice saying, "Taylor Swift sucks!" a voice called out from the road block. "We're coming over, don't shoot!"

No swiftie would be able to utter such a thing, let alone allow such an insult to go unpunished. Other human survivors had come.

As a precaution, they formed a defensive perimeter around Leigh. Watching the saviors walk over, they hoped for the best.

"Halt," called out Maura. "Friends wouldn't come around that corner. Enemies would."

The other group stopped. From the sound of the conversations and footsteps, Leigh could tell they were once more outnumbered.

"If we can stay armed but holster our weapons, will you do the same?" Maura asked.

"Agreed," said a woman's voice.

On the other side of the truck, the survivors met and greeted one another with big smiles and cheers following an initial tense stand-off.

"We don't have time to dilly-dally," said Mr. Bennett.

"Thanks for helping us out," said Maura. "We appreciate it."

"I figured," said one of the men. He was tall and gruesome, with a beard that hadn't been groomed for some time, if ever.

"There's a place for you back at our camp," said a large woman. She was wearing a floral muumuu. Her left arm was missing just below the elbow.

"Don't tell me y'all were heading north?" asked the bearded man.

"Not really," said Evan. "It's because of me. I have Lupus. I need help."

"I can't help you there, son." The bearded man turned his gaze to his group, signaling them to move out.

"We believe this man has a kind of immunity to the effects of the Taylor Swift album," said Mr. Bennett. "He claims to have been exposed and not changed from it. The incident itself was some time ago."

"We have a doctor. He might be able to run some tests. I'm Martin, by the way. It's good to see some more people. We have plenty of stuff to go around, so long as yer willin' to chip in and such."

"Of course," said Maura.

Everyone else introduced themselves in kind.

"That your daughter?" a gorgeous black woman named Kelly asked Maura. Her hair was curly and cut short.

"Oh no. I wish. She's wonderful."

Leigh blushed.

They walked for a few hours, stopping at a lumber yard to bring back as much firewood as they could carry. Then they headed to Martin's camp. It wasn't really a camp, but an old facility that had actually been abandoned long before

Taylor Swift took things over. It seemed like an excellent stronghold, even with the few openings where windows used to be. Martin and his people had boarded-up most of it and bragged about finding solar panels that provided rudimentary electricity for their needs. The building was constructed of red bricks and seemed amazing to Leigh. Due to its size, she wondered how they were able to guard it all.

"This is what's best of all— we're pretty far off the beaten path," said Martin. "The highway's so far off. We've haven't had to deal with swifties out here. Not yet, at least." As they walked through the fence, Leigh felt this place was safer than the mountains they had stayed in. "There's even a tiny view of Nashville a few floors up. Want to check it out?"

"Sure," said Leigh.

"I'll pass," said Evan. "I want to sleep."

Martin and three others from his group led Leigh, Mr. Bennett, and Maura up the dilapidated steps to the roof of the building. They saw Nashville as a far off glimmer of light.

"Looks more or less the same to me," said Martin.

"I've never actually seen it," said Maura.

"It's never going to be the same again," said Mr. Bennett.

"I'm not so sure about that," said a new voice. A woman joined them, looking in her mid-thirties with jet-black hair and pale skin. She was holding a cigarette.

"What do you mean?" asked Leigh.

Maura looked the woman over. Her eyes widened. "Hey, you're—"

"Yeah, yeah," said the woman. "Katy Perry."

SIX

It was unnerving for Leigh just how comfortable she had become living with Martin and the others. The compound had previously been a sanitarium for children. She was growing attached to the place, deluding herself into thinking the days of wandering around looking at relics of smashed fluorescent lighting and chalkboards filled with doodles from the hands of insane youths would become her life. A passive existence where food came easily enough, and there was a roof over her head. The truth was that at any moment, the swifties could come and take even more away from her.

Then she realized that if the swifties didn't ever come, the old issue of her carrying on the human race would come up once more. There were a few men she'd met at the compound which she found herself attracted to, but they were men, much older than she was. The youngest person besides herself was a boy named Al, and he was twenty-two years old. If the conditions were agreeable, being paired with Al wouldn't be so bad. But still, she had no interest in being a mother. She would run away before that was forced upon her.

Katy and the others had given them the date and time Leigh and the others had arrived: March 7th, 2023. One morning a few weeks later, Leigh knew she was fifteen. Leigh hadn't told anyone it was her birthday. Instead, she contemplated on the birthdays she'd had before.

The best one had to have been her sixth birthday. Her parents had taken her and her friends to play laser tag. They had pizza. She got dolls. There was so much laughter. Leigh's father played laser tag like a goofball. After, all of her friends had slept over and they made prank phone calls.

Not too long after that, Leigh had watched her mother kill her father. Maybe he was abusive, but Leigh never saw him do anything that would suggest something like that. The end of the world must have seemed like a good excuse for Leigh's mother. It even seemed congruent with Taylor Swift's ideology. The end of patriarchies, women everywhere seizing control. While they were running away from their home, the entire neighborhood was going up in flames. Leigh and her parents ran up a concrete stairwell adjacent to a bridge out of town. Her father being first in line. When he reached the top, he was still running, and her mother jumped over the last steps to push him into the lake below using the momentum. It happened without warning, and Leigh's mother grabbed Leigh's wrist to keep running. If Leigh's mother had an explanation, Leigh never heard it, because two days later, swifties had them trapped in a basement. Her mother sacrificed herself so Leigh could get away. Leigh had waited until the swifties were in the basement, not even understanding what they were then. She made for the streets above, her mother distracting the swifties.

Mr. Bennett had found her the next day, shell-shocked and starving. He had introduced himself as Liam. It wasn't until they joined up with Trevor, Evan, Zachary, and Maura that he insisted she call him Mr. Bennett.

She never got it, but he said it was to trigger a sense of normalcy for both of them. He'd lost his students, she'd lost her teachers. Leigh did as she was told, even if she didn't understand it.

"Hey, Leigh?" Evan asked as she stared off at Nashville's brightness. There was still electricity there.

She was pulled from her memories and met eyes with Evan, who was looking worried. "Hey. Any word from the doctor?"

"He's actually just a pre-med student. Still seemed on point, though. I mean, everyone else calls him Doctor Riley. All I need is some more medication he doesn't have, and I'll be fine. So, more or less, we're where we left off."

"We'll have to keep looking then. With all these people to help, I'm sure those swifties won't stand a chance if we can figure out a way to use your immunity to our advantage."

"Yeah." Evan sighed. "Look, we all need to sit down and talk. Plan our next move. Katy and Martin, they have ideas.."

"Okay, sure."

"But Leigh, I just want you to know. You're a strong girl, Leigh. I don't think I would have handled things as well when I was your age."

"Just wait until I'm your age," Leigh jested. "I'll be kicking more ass than Maura. And you'll be there to see it!" The time at the compound had made Leigh see just how important Evan could be. How worth fighting for. It was due to the slightest bit of community at the old building. If they could only take back the world, make it as great as the compound was everywhere else.

"I hope so."

The time came. Leigh and her group sat down with Martin, Katy, and others from Martin's camp in a defunct classroom.

"Katy's just the kind of person who likes to cut to the chase," Martin explained to Leigh. "She knows what she wants and how to get it."

Katy stood before Leigh while Maura, Evan, and Mr. Bennett paced around.

"We argued about this back and forth," Mr. Bennett said to Leigh. "She thinks you can make things normal. Save the world."

"Okay, but how?" asked Leigh.

"When things got heavy," Katy said, "the swifties considered me a high-profile target. Not just because they thought I used to have some trivial feud with Taylor, but because I could piece together exactly how she had precipitated her ascension. That I could replicate it to become an even greater threat. Sadly for her, I was able to escape California. She had wanted to take over the world for some time now. That is a common ambition for most pop stars. But we fulfill that desire figuratively. Taylor found a way to do so literally. And now she's the only one left standing."

"Yeah," said Leigh. "And the world is damaged goods."

"That hasn't been proven yet," said Katy. "In fact, we've been doing tests that suggest under certain circumstances, a reversal towards humanity might be possible in the case of a swiftie. Taylor's mind control is solely from the music she produced, especially her 2019 recordings. That means any deaf person who wasn't killed during the initial attacks are as immune as you believe Evan is. Now, as for her older music, well, it helped her blow up when she was younger. It doesn't have the potential to do anything but get stuck in your head. That doesn't change people into swifties like her newer material. The new mixes of them do, but when they were first released, they didn't. Back then, Taylor was innocent, naive, and adorable. I think if we utilize these attributes in you, we could potentially reverse the process. Restore the world back to the way it was."

"The debate is if swifties are still people or if they're too far gone," Dr. Riley said between jotting down notes from the meeting. "In order words, could they regain their humanity, their rationality? Which is why we want to further our research with you as a volunteer. Let Katy teach you."

"But I don't understand," said Leigh, motioning her arms to Katy. "You want to make me like Taylor? I don't want to be like Taylor."

"You don't have to be," said Martin. "You could be better. Reinstall governments and order. Stabilize the population. Give people back their free will."

"What's it going to take?"

"Seriously," said Maura to Katy. "It sounds like bullshit to me."

"We're going to use the foundations and techniques Taylor employed in her music, only amplify them," elaborated Katy. "Perhaps have the lyrics be about something less trite yet even more relatable than boys and breakups. You and every human left in this world have the same experience of being a hunted minority. That right there is trauma, and that's where real art comes from. Families have been abolished in the swiftie culture. With my own experiences as a chart-topping musician, I think we can subvert Taylor's rule and make things right. Leigh has to write it, though. It has to be music with feeling, and she has to mean it."

"You really think a new song by Leigh will turn swifties back to normal human beings?" asked Evan.

"Yes, but it has to be good. That's how we take over."

"So you could trump Swift's influence and lead things yourself?" Leigh questioned, her hostility apparent.

"No, Leigh. I just want to go back to the way things were. Even worse than the norm would be acceptable. People deserve free will." Katy looked down at her gray rainjacket. "This is the last nice thing I own. That part of my life is done with. I just don't want to eke out my days in this building while there's still a chance we can try to fix this. But it's up to you, Leigh."

"What about Evan? He needs medication. Will you help him?"

"I'm not a priority," Evan said to Katy.

"Evan, I don't want to lose you," Leigh said, her voice low.

"We'll do what we can," said Martin. "But you need to understand there are no guarantees in any of this. We're just guessing based on insufficient data."

"Hence why we need more swifties to experiment on," said Mr. Bennett.

"That won't be an issue," said Katy. She focused her attention back on Leigh. "If you agree, you'll need to do as I say. I'll expect your complete commitment. It won't be easy, as you're the last hope for humanity. I'll teach you everything I know, but you need to be willing to learn."

"Tell her everything, Katy," said Maura. "Where it ends."

"The end game is to have you record some music. I have a loose network of human contacts waiting for a positive result on returning a swiftie into a human. Pending that, we coordinate an assault on Nashville, using my engineer to patch the speaker hub at the Tayloradium— that's the source of Taylor's music being broadcast through the city on speakers. If we can switch it out with your performance, it's a start. Then we make it out like she's passing on power to you. Maybe if we're lucky we can coordinate it with other major cities to do the same. Keep in mind, though, this might be a one-way mission, even if we succeed. And even that is contingent on your ability to rise to the occasion."

"Katy," said Leigh. "It's fine. I'm in."

The first lesson for Leigh was listening to Katy's music. She enjoyed it, though not as much as the 90's compilation CD.

"I wrote very conceptual songs," Katy explained, standing over Leigh as the girl felt strange."They were catchy in a different way than Taylor's, and certainly just as popular. They were written for a generation. That type of music becomes what your parents listened to. Some of it doesn't hold up as a result. It's old and unappealing. New pop sensations come in while others don't follow conventions. But now Taylor sets up numerous edicts to discourage any other type of music, effectively breaking the cycle."

"I've heard of those," said Leigh. "But what are they?"

"Good idea. If we're going to pull this off, we need to consider the edicts." Katy went over to a box and fished inside of it until she pulled out a piece of paper. She began reading:

"One: Men are both the source of all inspiration and all frustration. There should be as few of them as possible. The ones who are left will, therefore, be gracious and give us whatever we want.

"Two: By that same token, men and women should be equal. But due to centuries of subjugation and oppression, women will be the dominant gender during my reign as a means of compensation.

"Three: No smoking and no movies with smoking in them allowed. Eww!

"Four: Every one of my fans is special. Spreading my music and message will make the world more special."

"She makes it seem so polite," said Leigh.

"That was her image. The paragon of sweet, successful, and happy." Katy read on. "Five: Not that I ever thought or wanted to rule the known universe, but now that I do, it's totally awesome. I do my best… so don't try to overthrow me, okay? I know my fans would never do such a thing, but we still have some enemies lingering.

"Six: God probably exists, but just in case, pray to me too.

"Seven: Music is important. But especially my music. Listening to my music every chance means so much to me. Not listening to anyone else's music means even more!" Katy looked up from the document and down at Leigh with a scowl." See, there are no rules forbidding the listening of other music besides her own. She simply emphasizes the importance of her own music, making it seem rude not to. Or even that it would be inconceivable not to.

"Eight: Though you may be tempted to kill my ex-boyfriends, and yours for that matter, realize that none of them deserve to be murdered in cold blood. Instead, send them to one of the Boyfriend Reeducation Centers where they can learn to be better." Katy grunted in disgust. "These are glorified internment camps. You think I'm bad with the swifties, you wouldn't want to step foot anywhere near one of these."

"Nine: Of course, feel free to kill the haters who don't love me. Shake it off long enough, and it'll be just me and my swifties forever!

"Ten: Make sure to read this everyday!!! I love you all."

"Jeez," said Leigh.

"I know, right? Now, let's backtrack to edict seven. It means the first song you record needs to be a Taylor Swift cover."

"What? Have you consulted with Maura and the others about that?"

"You said you were willing to do whatever it takes. They have no say in your decisions anymore. We have one chance. We have to make it seem as if Taylor is bequeathing her title to you. The swifties will be pacified. That's when we'll play the second song, something original of yours that we'll need to pull out of you. That's what I think will jar the swifties enough to bring them back."

"But I don't want to become a swiftie in the process!" Leigh protested.

"You won't."

"How am I supposed to learn one of Taylor's songs if listening to it turns me, Katy?"

"That's not the present issue. We have to carefully study all the tracks on the Taylor Swift album that first caused all of this. The one with "Even Without High Heels." In the meantime, you can't even sing. You're shit. We have a lot of work to do." Katy then made Leigh run for an hour in order to learn how to control her breathing. Leigh nearly collapsed. That was the first but not the last time Katy laid down the hammer on Leigh.

The Detrimental Effect of Taylor Swift's Music on Human Autonomy
By Gregory Riley

Abstract: In the year 2019, Taylor Swift unleashed an album which programmed the populous to do her bidding. They became obsessed, irrationally driven fans who did whatever she said. This report chronicles the experiments performed on two swiftie test subjects to ascertain how this music could possibly have such a profound effect on the human psyche, and if there is a way to turn a swiftie back into a normal functioning human being with their autonomy intact.

Most likely, it is an auditory phenomenon, as those hard of hearing seem less susceptible and people who are deaf are immune from the phenomenon. Thus it is, by deduction, something present in the Taylor Swift songs that were added in post-production.

The methods used include psychological evaluations, prolonged isolation, and non-stop exposure to other music besides the aforementioned Taylor Swift album. Subjects captured are still unable to respond to questions and grasp the English language. Swifties in isolation exhibit much less cognitive function than swifties in groups, i.e. ones who have regular access to both Taylor Swift and Taylor Swift's music. Several imprinting methods attempted in hopes of finding a trace of consciousness. Still no postive results.

SEVEN

"And this, well, this is… we call him Ceecee," said Katy.

Leigh stood a few paces behind Katy as she unveiled the swifties she was holding captive. "Really inventive, Ms. Perry."

"Ms. Perry, huh? I didn't ask you to call me that."

"Oh. Mr. Bennett does, and you're more of a teacher to me than him. Do you not like it?"

"It's weird. But call me what you want. It's what everyone else does."

Leigh was fairly indifferent to Ceecee as she looked the swiftie over. Under the tatters of his filthy clothing was an emaciated body. Above that was long, unkempt hair. Ceecee was like a feral animal, his range of motion limited by a chain attached to a post in the rear parking lot of the old hospital. Compared to Aye, the first swiftie Katy had shown Leigh (who had been tortured nearly to death via waterboarding and was much more docile than any swiftie Leigh had seen before) and the second, Beebee, a woman, Ceecee didn't seem to be kept in quite as poor condition as the others. She questioned Katy about this.

"Ceecee has been showing some impressive progress towards re-humanization."

"How so?" Leigh saw feces stains on the male swiftie's left heel as he napped under a shady tree.

"Don't worry about it. Suffice it to say it's still more swiftie than human. That's why you need to step things up, Leigh. Remember what we talked about?"

"All of it," Leigh said, her tone defensive.

"Bullshit. What's the relative minor of D#?"

Leigh let out a series of stammering "Um's."

"Christ, kid."

"Yeah, but the relative minor of C is—"

"Everyone knows the relative minor of C!"

"I'm sorry, I'm doing my best, Katy."

"Forgot it. We're not here to figure out you're full of shit. I have to know more about your troubles, your suffering. I will bring it out if I have to. We don't have a lot of time left. How does this Ceecee make you feel?"

"Like my parents are dead."

"Do you believe in heaven and hell?" Katy asked.

"I don't know."

"Figure it out, it's not hard. God would not make the Antichrist Taylor Swift. Hell just happens, Leigh. You're never going to see your parents again."

"I know. And I'm trying really hard to do what you tell me to."

"It's not going to be enough. You have to feel it. Give me more. Smell Ceecee and his puke. Reconcile the fact that there is no afterlife. The more you can channel your suffering, the more likely you'll be able to reach the swifties and turn them back."

"What have you done to Ceecee to help him?" asked Leigh. "Just what progress has he made that isn't good enough for him to have to live outside like this?"

"You don't understand. My life is devoted to helping swifties recover. It starts with Ceecee."

"So you just let him rot in his own filth?"

"Don't sympathize with the enemy. He is the enemy until he's human again. You expect us to clean him? When he'd claw our throats out and moan Taylor Swift lyrics into the open hole?"

"Whatever," said Leigh.

Leigh paid for her attitude. Another long run around the compound with Katy behind her on a bike trying to chase her. Leigh's resolve ran out once the run was over, but the day still went on.

They soon returned to the old classroom, and Katy throttled her for more information, probing deeper into Leigh's being.

It was a trial by fire each day, alternations between foundational elements of creation and Leigh's own motivations as a prospective artist. How to appeal to a massive audience. Where falsetto was inappropriate. Why taste was subjective.

"Why do people make art?" Katy asked Leigh on one of those days.

"They're bored," Leigh said, answering Katy as if it were obvious.

"That's too simple, Leigh. They're destitute. Missing something. They feel the need to bring that lack into existence. Often, what is manifested is useless, what the person really needed was a hug. But it can't come from nothing. I don't care what they say. So where does it come from?"

"Inside?" Leigh asked, her mind drained. She'd almost missed the question. Her loathing toward Katy grew more and more each day. Leigh supposed that was all part of Katy's agenda, but still. Her former privilege as a celebrity made her cantankerous and unreasonable. Yet it wasn't as if Leigh could quit.

"And out, Leigh. Don't be foolish. Art is a process. We all *suffer*. No matter who you are. Something is eating away at you. Something is *always* missing. Art is the shallow answer to our suffering. Art is the conversion of our suffering into something beautiful. Memorable. Useful. Evocative."

"Okay?"

Katy snatched the pages Leigh had been writing on from the desk into her outstretched hands. "So why are your lyrics making me suffer when they're supposed to be moving my soul into a unanimous harmony?"

"Katy, stop it, I'm trying. I don't have the same mind as

you. I can't do what you do!" Leigh protested.

"Taylor and I made song after song turning our suffering into beauty. Positive angles from negative circumstances. It's simple. You just have to relate to people. Common experiences, Leigh. Think of all the people your age hypnotized by Taylor Swift. Imagine the feeling of them descending into the form of swifties, knowing they were losing their minds and spirits. You've lost your autonomy too, as a result. You can't go to the movies or the amusement park. Why won't you channel that?"

"I am. I cannot stand to be around you. It's making things more difficult for me to do what you ask."

"Overcome it. It's a struggle!" Katy tore up Leigh's latest song. "I'm getting fed up with you too. I have a harder job than you. Understand what's at stake. Try again, Leigh. Something entirely new. I don't want a song about heartbreak with the emotional investment of melted ice cream. I need power in your words. Make me feel them! You need to become a better lyricist."

"But you had co-writers, producers, help! You're just forcing a pencil into my face and watching my every fuck-up!"

"Just give up," said Katy. "Take your role in this new world as the final generation of man. Go breed and watch the swifties take your children away and blow your brains out. That's what the world expected of women. To make fucking babies. Now you have a chance to be more. Prove your mettle on your own. I can't fucking hold your hand. You need to be the best to beat Taylor because that's how most of the world thinks of her."

"If that's what it's going to take, then that's what I'll be," Leigh insisted.

There was an announcement coming from the intercom. At first, Leigh ignored it, knowing a true emergency would involve everyone flocking to her room (a third floor Meter

Room with a small cot that she found to be comfortable) but before she fell back into her much-needed sleep, she realized something. What was being said on the intercom throughout the building? It was her writing. Her diary.

"Katy Perry is a…"

The damage might have already been done, but nonetheless, Leigh raced from the bed to where Katy was broadcasting Leigh's secrets to the entire compound, down two flights of stairs then flying through the hallway, Leigh remembered what she'd written as it was recited to her.

"Dear Juan, you're probably long gone. All of my family's gone. You're gone. I'm still here for some reason, trying to fix things. But nothing will fix me but you. I never even got to telling you I wanted you."

Leigh's legs pumped faster, feeling heavier and heavier as Katy read on mercilessly. She was skipping around as if she'd read the worst most savory parts of her diary beforehand and was playing them off like a greatest hits album.

"Still, no one knows my biggest secret— my name is actually Leif. You remember, Juan? Pronounced *laif*. I'm not a Viking! I love being able to write whatever I want. So that's not who I am… my stupid mother naming me ridiculous things. Not even a girl's name, no. It's supposed to mean something. You called me Leigh. You said it was because the alphabet is flexible sometimes. You kept my secret. I'm so afraid of forgetting you."

Thankfully, Leigh did not encounter anyone until she was outside of the office. Two guards stood out front and held Leigh back at each attempt she made to pass them. One of them with a free hand spoke into his walkie-talkie to Katy saying, "She's here."

"Al's such a cutie, though…" Katy stopped reading. The guards let Leigh enter, and Leigh walked in on Katy smiling. Leigh swiped the diary out of Katy's hand.

"Why!?" Leigh exclaimed.

"No celebrity deserves to keep secrets," said Katy. "Not

if you're just going to leave them lying around."

It was Ceecee who proved Katy's theory right. What made Leigh anxious was how the woman could have known.

Aye, BeeBee, and Ceecee were brought to every studio session, and under heavy supervision. This gave Leigh a chance to insist they were well-groomed. Katy obliged Leigh, with the only stipulation being that Leigh be the one who cleaned the swifties. Leigh faltered briefly, but out of spite, she cleaned the swifties before she and Katy practiced each day.

The Taylor Swift song Katy chose for Leigh to do a cover of was "Blank Space." All three of the swifties reacted positively. They sang along as best as they could. Leigh worked on it, again and again, using Katy's knowledge from when the song was constantly played on the radio. That's when Katy would sing her songs to the swifties. Smack them and ask them for their human names. Leigh could tell by their reactions that it went from seeming to be a heresy to passive acceptance. They knew listening to Katy was forbidden, but they began to enjoy it without guilt. To disregard the edicts. The breakthrough came a few weeks after Leigh's struggle to write a song Katy would accept to produce with the hypnotizing beats.

Ceecee, after being asked hundreds of times by Katy over a period of months, finally answered one of her questions. It was unexpected, as Katy and Leigh were trying to harmonize their voices for song and it happened without warning. Leigh hadn't realized who the voice was, but Katy immediately ran over to him as Ceecee spoke in a dazed mutter.

"Tell me again," Katy asked him.

"Dale… it's Dale… Dale Amicus."

EIGHT

Maura's room was in the basement of the compound. As the time was fast approaching in which Leigh would be finishing the final parts of the recordings they'd attempt to play city-wide from the Tayloradium, Leigh found herself increasingly restless. Hoping Maura would be awake as she usually was, Leigh walked slowly towards the woman's room. It was covered only by a dusty blue bed sheet that did not even reach to the floor. It sounded as if she was awake because there were noises coming from inside. Sexual ones.

Eavesdropping, Leigh became shocked to discover a conversation taking place between breaths and moans. The subject was of no consequence to her, some lamenting about how much they each missed the Internet after Taylor Swift had shut it down in an attempt to eliminate sources in which other music could be found. It was who Maura was with that mattered to Leigh.

It was Al. The only boy in years she'd wanted anything to do with. And Maura was having her way with him. As silently as she could, Leigh departed back to her room, feeling the lump in her throat and trying to push it down, knowing she would have to try to channel that pain into her songwriting rather than wallowing in a familiar sorrow.

Bouts of troubled sleep increased following Leigh's discovery. One night, when she finally did fall asleep, someone entered her room and woke her up.

"What's going on?" asked Leigh as the lights came on.

"Leigh. I have something you should know." It was Katy. With her, his arms trussed in rope was Mr. Bennett.

"What's he doing here?" Leigh wondered.

"Leigh, do you know what a pedophile is?" asked Katy.

"Yeah. I think so."

"Do you know Mr. Bennett was one? That he raped two of his students years back?"

"What?" Leigh's voice became high-pitched in astonishment.

"Two girls. Even younger than you." Katy kicked Mr. Bennett onto the ground. He was unable to brace his fall. Saying nothing, he only grimaced after he was on the ground.

"What the fuck," said Leigh. She scratched her chin then pulled her hair behind her ears. "Did something just happen?"

"Yeah. I just found out," said Katy. She let out a cynical sneer. "That's why the others told you to call him Mr. Bennett. As a reminder to him not to fuck with you. Maura recognized him from when he was on the news. What I want to know is, did he ever try to touch you, Leigh? Tell the truth, and we'll make him pay. That's what they used to do to pedophiles. This shit-head nearly got off scot-free."

"I don't really qualify losing my career and my reputation scot-free," said Mr. Bennett.

"No!" shouted Leigh. "Mr. Bennett took care of me. He was annoying in his lectures at times, but he saved me."

"You better be thankful for Maura, who really saved you. Are you sure he never tried anything when you were alone? Do you just not want to tell me?"

"Stop." Leigh couldn't move from out of her bed.

"He's been thinking about you all this time, I bet. Weighing his options. A lot of girls who've been assaulted— I know they don't want to talk about it."

"He never touched me," Leigh said, fully awake now. "Do whatever you want with him, but he didn't do anything to me."

"Maybe he felt you up when you were asleep one of those nights. Knocked out from a long day on the road. Leigh. How do you know?"

"Katy. Please. We have a hell of a day tomorrow."

"Fine. But please let me know if anything happened. I'm here for you." Somehow, Leigh didn't buy that. And she sensed Katy knew that too.

As Leigh scarfed down her mashed potatoes, Maura asked her, "Why have you been such a bitch lately?" They were sitting on the floor in Maura's room.

"Real mature, Maura," countered Leigh.

"Seriously. Talk to me, hun."

"Did you know I liked Al? Did Katy encourage you to seduce him or something? I don't understand, Maura."

"Al. Ah, shit. I don't know, kiddo."

"I thought you loved Zachary."

"Leigh, he's gone. What do you want me to do? Stay faithful to him?"

"I don't know. Hook up with someone I don't like? That was wrong, okay?"

"I am sorry, then," said Maura.

"You know, I used to think you guys were going to make me breed. You know, to like continue the human race or something?"

"It crossed all of our minds, Leigh. I mean, you were the only one out of us who could."

"What about you?"

Maura let out a sigh. "I have PCOS." Maura rose up and went into her backpack, in search of something.

"What's that?"

"It means my hormones are out of balance. Scientific details aside, my chances of bearing children are slim to none. Look, never mind that. I mean we've got a better plan for you. There are plenty of girls left who can be mothers. No one would force you, especially with your new role in things." Maura returned to Leigh's side and showed her a glass bottle with a rolled-up piece of paper inside. "A few birthdays back, Zachary gave me this. He said to open it if anything ever happened to him."

"Wow, Maura. That was so thoughtful of him."

"Not exactly. He was simple but sweet. It's not the kind of thing I appreciated, even now. That's why I haven't opened it. It's not going to be enough, whatever it says, you know?"

"I would have cracked it open five seconds after he was gone," said Leigh. "I would have gone straight for it."

"I might never see what it says. If it's going to be enough to break my heart, I don't know if I want that. People are gone. I don't need messages from the dead. I just want to accept it and keep going."

"But you still hold onto it?" asked Leigh. Maura had a way of communicating that Leigh couldn't seem to fully understand. It was like Maura knew what to say to gain Leigh's forgiveness so easily.

"Call it a crutch. Besides, if I'm ever dead to rights, maybe I'll feel differently about it. That's how I want to go out. I want my last few minutes to be seeing what the hell this lovable sap wrote to me."

That was their last night at the hospital compound. Katy planned to move their operations to a place where post-production of the tracks Leigh had recorded could take place, in conjunction with organizing the remnant of human outliers who hid away from the cities all dominated by swifties.

While the adults were meeting trying to pitch the plan to another group of survivors, Leigh flipped through a notebook of Katy's and saw the track list of the Taylor Swift album which had precipitated things:

Another Milestone
Taylor Swift

Single Release of "Even Without High Heels": January 7th, 2019
Release date of the release date: August 12th, 2019
Release date: February 30th, 2020
1. Intro
2. I'm Not Brainwashing You
3. The Loneliest Onlyest
4. Still Thin
5. Cartwheel in the Prairie
6. Even Without High Heels
7. Rejecting Yourself
8. I'm Not Basic (You're Just Complicated)
9. I Brought My Fans Pizza, They Brought Me An Earthquake
10. Love Song I Wrote About You For My Fans

When the meeting was over, Leigh asked Katy, "How are the recordings supposed to work? If they utilize the same nature of beats as these songs, how is that re-humanization possible? Won't it just shift their imperatives and loyalty from Taylor Swift to me?"

"It's a step forward. Instead of being executed, Mr. Bennett has volunteered to be a test subject to see what happens when a human listens to the final master tracks of your music."

There were many outtakes, but Katy put most of her focus on three songs, as that would be all they would have time for. The first one they would play was Taylor Swift's "Blank Space." Then a song co-written by Katy Perry and Leigh called "The Talking." The last was the one Leigh had done almost entirely on her own titled "Meager."

"Incidentally, so has Dale, but we have forbidden him to for obvious reasons."

Dale Amicus had proven Katy's hunch to be correct. He'd only listened to the demos of Leigh's recordings, and it had, after a long enough period of time, caused him to snap out of it and reclaim his identity and memories. The gratitude he felt towards Leigh was more like reverence, making Leigh feel uneasy.

Eventually, Katy's recruitment for humans and support became more dangerous than fruitful as the further they strayed from the compound, the more swifties they'd encountered. That's when they settled on finally orchestrating their assault on Nashville, feeling the weight of all humanity on their shoulders.

PART THREE

"Death seduces generations"
-Schoolyard Heroes

NINE

Just outside of their objective in the community of Green Hills, Leigh and the other human allies waited for Katy's signal. It had taken six days of itching and circumventing the perimeter Taylor Swift had set up around her kingdom formerly known as Nashville.

Outside of the multitude of swifties they'd encountered (most of whom were female), Leigh was surprised how well things around her appeared the closer they got to Nashville proper. The streets were clean, the buildings were being repaired, and the occasional swiftie road crew was clearing abandoned cars off the streets. There had been unfathomable chaos when Taylor Swift vied for her throne —fires, looting, and death were all prevalent, and all of it to the soundtrack of her music. With a loss of conflict against a declining human population, Nashville was able to undergo reconstruction, and Leigh believed it was probably happening in other cities as well. It hurt their cause in a way since they were technically going to do what Taylor Swift did in the first place. Katy rationalized it in terms of the minds of the captive swifties, with Dale as the prime example of a possible return to normalcy someday. Aye and Beebee had also exhibited a few features of a returning human intellect after undergoing a similar process that Dale had. Their language was fragmented, and they did not know their own names or what a name was, but they were making progress each day. All thanks to Leigh.

In total, Katy wasn't able to find more than a few hundred humans in the distances they'd traveled around in hopes of a coordinated speaker hijacking. It was all she could muster. That force was divided into four equally split divisions, two of which were spear-heading a direct assault on Nashville, another coming in on the Cumberland River as another means of disorientation for the swifties, and then the division whose task was to get Leigh setup at the Tayloradium, which was located in downtown Nashville. Their position in Green Hills had not resulted in any action or defensive maneuvers from the swifties as of yet. There were sentries on a watertower behind the cul-de-sac looking in the direction of Katy's planned distraction. All was still calm from their reports.

Besides the dozens of people she didn't know, with her were Evan, Dr. Riley, Martin, Dale, and Ralph, the sound engineer who was going to patch the speaker hub to get Leigh's music to be played citywide. Then there was a short Asian woman with a ponytail named Martha, who reveled in every step forward they'd take. Upon introducing herself to Leigh, she also introduced her friend, a man named Brian who was balding and had a nice tan from farming on the compound.

Brian loved to talk. Leigh had heard his entire life story, for the most part, despite not listening and not being around him more than a few minutes at a time. He was smoking a stale cigarette and rambling on, "My sister was so gay!"

"But I don't get it, Brian," said Martha, a dubious expression on her face. "If she was so religious, how could she reconcile herself?"

"Oh, see, she couldn't. Said she was going to Hell. How'd you like that? Natalie's the only person I think I'll ever meet who is totally devout but thinks we're still damned. I mean, she got it anyway. Hey, you know Taylor Swift killed my mother?"

"You mean, like, indirectly?"

"No! I was visiting her in the TV room, right? Then Taylor Swift comes in, curly hair all frayed up and cuts her thumbs up, eats 'em, and then punched my fat old mother to death."

"How'd you know it was Taylor?" asked a young boy. He might have been younger than Leigh as he certainly was shorter. Leigh reminded herself never to condemn someone on that basis.

"She said, 'I'm Taylor Swift' right to me," said Brian. "That's when I recognized her. She said, 'I've come to kill your momma' and such."

Leigh felt it must have been a fabrication because Brian had no shortage of outrageous stories like that. Those who were not familiar with him, to their detriment, began to call him out on some of the details. His tactic was to become so exasperated, in scrutinizing person in question let it go.

Evan approached her, tapping Leigh on the head. "How are you doing, Leigh?"

"It's chilly out."

"Eh, it's not so bad," said Evan. "You just need to move around. I know it's hard since this is the first rest we've gotten all day."

"I guess. Hey, Evan?"

"Hmmm?"

"Trevor was really mean. An ass-aholic for sure. But not to you. Why'd he take such good care of you? Did he really save your life?"

"I guess so. I mean if I didn't turn into a swiftie, those swifties that had me held down would have probably killed me. I can't say for sure. After he had saved me, I think he just had a lot of sympathy for how sick I was. I was not ready for the end of the world. For the most part, I was immobile in my apartment. No one came for me so I couldn't move myself. Trevor told me he'd look after me until I started to turn, and then he'd give me a mercy killing. I accepted his proposal, and he'd bring me food and keep me safe. I never did turn, even though I'm sure those swifties forced me to listen to some of the songs that would have done the job. Before things had gotten so bad, Trevor was part of an

SHTF group.''

"What's that?" Leigh asked.

"Shit Hits The Fan. Doomsday preppers. He told me everyone had made fun of his local group. And that he'd had the last laugh when he was ready for what happened and they weren't. No, I agree with you. Trevor was really mean to most everybody. But even before that evidence that I could possibly be immune to the effects of the music's mind control, he showed me great kindness."

"Katy's really mean too. It all makes me wonder, you know?"

"It's like one of those things, Leigh," said Evan placidly. "Somebody's gotta be a dick, otherwise what would we have to talk about?"

"I don't follow you." But before Evan could go on, Martin strode over from the watertower to the curb where they were seated.

"It won't be long. Be ready to move out."

"Oh God," Leigh heard Martha say.

"About time," said Brian. "I'll kill this bitch myself!"

Leigh walked away simply to get away from Brian's obnoxious declarations. As she passed Mr. Bennett, they exchanged uncomfortable glances, and he continued practicing his shooting position. Mr. Bennett, like Dale, was surrounded by people according to Katy's specifications with orders to observe him and Dale for any aberrant behavior. Katy had initially wanted him not to go anywhere near Leigh, but he pleaded that he wished to protect her, and Leigh accepted his offer despite their warped relationship. The old man did genuinely care for Leigh. She just had no way of knowing in what way. Nonetheless, she knew he could only be a help to her if trouble came. As for his exposure to the music Leigh had recorded, it led him to exhibit similar qualities as the swifties, albeit with an obsession to Leigh, not Taylor. But Katy's refinements to the tracks in post-production had allowed for Mr. Bennett to remain human.

Not too far off from Mr. Bennett was a rehabilitated Dale, who everyone was interested in talking to. He greeted Leigh. The most important priority in evaluating Dale a few months back was to find out how he felt about Leigh. He described it as unbounded gratitude and a love for her music, but also a relief for the return of his free will.

"Just, on a personal basis, I'd probably do anything you say, Leigh. Even if that was not to do anything you say."

"You sure?" Katy, then Leigh had asked him continuously.

"Positive, sugar."

"Do you feel any similar feelings to me that you did to Taylor?" Leigh asked him one day a few weeks back. "I just want to understand because… if this works, I don't want to be like her. I want things to be normal. I want to be normal and just live my life."

The guards that surrounded him had orders to consider him unsafe, but given the fact that he used to be foaming at the mouth with garbled syllables of Taylor Swift lyrics, Leigh felt he'd never voluntarily become a swiftie. Once that was settled, they asked him about his time under Taylor's massively destructive influence.

By all accounts, it seemed to be a largely unconscious existence with an occasionally conscious objective to listen and obey whatever came directly from Taylor herself. Some were charged with the defense of Nashville while others were left to their own devices. Leigh thought it wouldn't be so bad living in Nashville as a swiftie. Mostly because the concept of "bad" was merely something Dale hadn't recognized as a swiftie. The appearance of solidarity and the joy Taylor showed them was all he needed. It was automatic — let Taylor in, and there was no worrying about getting by, hunger, or homelessness. There would be much less struggle. And of course, Leigh would have to be responsible for ruining it all. And if not, Taylor Swift would devour her, torture her, execute her in the most savage way possible.

There were all kinds of cruel and unusual punishments permitted under Taylor Swift's regime. And to Leigh's reckoning what they were trying to do was probably the worst sin imaginable to the swifties.

Leigh once more crossed eyes with Mr. Bennett. He nodded to her. She nodded back but her face crinkled, and she turned away. Why couldn't Maura have come with them instead of him? She'd given Leigh Zachary's Glock with the hope she'd use it more than he ever did.

Knowing Mr. Bennett better than most, Evan and Leigh were supposed to be the ones to report any fluctuations in his behavior to the isolation detail assigned to him, but Leigh paid little attention to the molester, deferring all of those duties to Evan.

The sky lit up. There were loud noises, crashing objects. The world around Leigh was no longer still.

"Move out!" someone called out.

Those who had bikes, such as Leigh, mounted them and assimilated into the innermost section of walking humans as they moved towards the center of Taylor Swift's kingdom.

Five of the soldiers surrounding Leigh were down before they all found cover behind a shed. More of the human forces began converging on the rendezvous point now since Katy had made her move a distance away. It only took fifteen minutes after they'd left the watertower to encounter swifties. At first, it had been easy. Some of the soldiers broke off and killed them quickly. Then they reached a community of swifties, seemingly in hiding until a hoard of them erupted from the homes and attacked.

"PUSH FORWARD!" commanded someone at the front.

"No. We need cover!" exclaimed Mr. Bennett.

As shaken and terrified as Leigh was (she couldn't hear any Taylor Swift music coming from the speakers on the street signs, but they had been prepared for the fact that

Nashville's speaker system supposedly played Taylor Swift nonstop), she disagreed with Mr. Bennett. There was no point in cover when the objective was getting to Katy. The gauntlet had to be run.

In a series of gunshots and grenades, Leigh and the others defeated an entire neighborhood, but the commotion quickly drew attention to the fact that there was a force of humans attacking Nashville.

Up ahead were more people, and they signaled back to indicate they were humans, not swifties. At that point, the people around Leigh were walking at a fast enough pace that she and the others on bicycles could pedal forward and remained balanced. Even from a distance and with ear plugs on, the sounds from Katy's position felt like they were cracking the frame of Leigh's delicate body, and they were only getting closer.

Eventually, they did find themselves pinned down beyond Donelson near a cemetery and train tracks. There were swifties of every variety pulling up in cars, trying to run Leigh and her division down, causing them to flee into the cemetery.

"Not exactly a promising place to retreat," said Evan. His breathing was uneven, and soon, he began heaving. "I wouldn't mind tapping out about now."

"No! Evan, we're so damn close," said Leigh. But they waited for more help from the division on the river and the swifties at the cemetery were defeated. Leigh and the others advanced, having lost most of the people they'd started out with. To Leigh's relief, Brian had been shot several times in the chest, presumably by a swiftie. There were only a few miles left to the Tayloradium, but before that, they'd converged upon Katy's position. The sounds, which had been roaring and intense since Leigh and the others had advanced were dying down. Whatever diversion Katy had planned was coming to an end, for better or for worse.

TEN

Soot and dust dominated Leigh's field of vision as her protectors continued to push through the countless swifties driving off the I-40 exit right above them. It seemed the swifties had completely cleared Nashville of all the abandoned traffic and reallocated the vehicles to the swifties that came to Nashville like Muslims had to Mecca a long time ago.

The division of men and woman backing Leigh's safe arrival to the Tayloradium were slowing their advance in response to the decreased numbers and further opposition. They remained bold, however, as just beyond the underpass a few yards away was the rendezvous point with Katy and the other divisions. Leigh was escorted to different buildings amongst a series of thin apartment complexes where she and the others would enter and gun down the charging swifties. Seeing a male swiftie in the crowd, Leigh actually lamented his death when he was knocked over by bullets to his chest. There weren't enough males left to kill them so carelessly. But what other option did they have?

As they crested the steps of another apartment building, Martha signaled everyone to a halt and then called out something as loud as she could. Leigh couldn't make out what she'd said between the chaos outside and her ear protection.

One of the soldiers Leigh had recognized from the compound kept moving a bit longer than the rest of the line. It was Oscar, who'd deliberately caused himself to go deaf following his escape from New Orleans without his family.

"The speakers— no one's heard them this entire time,"

said Martha, daring to pull the protection out of her ears.

"So?" asked a man. "They're probably just going to switch them on as soon as you call to take your blast plugs out!"

"No," said Mr. Bennett. "You've all seen the speakers as we've walked the streets. There's even some in the building. I think it's a sign that Katy's gotten further than planned."

"I doubt that," said Martha.

"Then the alternative would be they are silencing the speakers for our arrival. Which, tactically, makes little sense to me."

"Maybe their tactician is a swiftie," one of the squad leaders suggested.

"Don't be foolish," said Martin. "We know Taylor has some human advisers still. What do you make of it, Dale?"

"I make nothin' out of it," said Dale.

"Everyone, leave your ear protection out at your own risk," said the squad leader. "Those who are willing to chance it will perform the job of our ears."

"But please," urged Martin, "for God's sake, be ready to put them back on as soon as you hear anything coming through the speakers. It could be Leigh's recordings but no need to chance it."

The sun was receding from view, compelling Leigh's group to get past the remaining swiftie opposition. They accomplished the task, but not without a massive loss of life. Leigh watched as complete strangers willingly came to her side or took the lead directly ahead of her in the gap where the last person protecting her had fallen. When Martin took up one of the spots, Leigh knew their numbers were running low, as Martin was fairly high up in the chain of command. Leigh turned her head for just a moment, and he was down. Dr. Riley attempted to drag him to a safer spot away from the line of fire, but Martin commanded him to move on with the others.

The isolation detail on Mr. Bennett and Dale was

consolidated into ten, then eight. It continued shrinking. From what Leigh could see, Dale had no compunction about killing swifties, and that seemed to give everyone else more hope.

The downfall of the swifties was they just didn't have enough brain function for proper aim. Leigh herself never could figure out her shaking problem, one that persisted no matter how much Maura trained her, but the swifties barely even held their guns properly. They simply remained snarling while singing some Taylor Swift song over and over again. No amount of direction from their leader could resolve their vacuous minds.

In a lull between fights, Leigh looked over a folded brochure one of the soldiers had found on a rack outside of a convenience store. It was for one of those boyfriend places Katy had told her about, occuring early on after Taylor seized power, before the swifties completely lost their minds. Leigh opened it up to pictures of groups of men sitting at desks, and read the contents:

Hey loves, it's Taylor! So I need to talk to you about something serious— our rapidly declining male population. I know I said men are bad, and I stick by it, but that doesn't mean we can't make them better. They just don't understand us girls. Point being, I have a new solution instead of just killing our negligent boyfriends.

All over the world, I have refurbished old churches to serve as Boyfriend Reeducation Centers. Just bring your boyfriend, husband, or significant other that identifies as male to one of these locations, and for however long it takes, my staff will instruct them on how to treat you right.

They'll be given the equivalent pains of menstruations through the process, as this has been found to best foster a sense of understanding. But we also teach things like when to clip their toenails and how to notice and compliment new haircuts.

The thing is, I really don't abide by all these killings, you should only kill someone if they're not one of my fans. But even then, you should do your best to show them how much fun we have and how much we love one another so they can join us.

Now lately, I've been getting really uneasy about this, but I think this is a practical solution to a longstanding problem. Men are just completely unsympathetic to our female condition. These programs will educate them and teach them how to care for both themselves and for you.

This is by no means mandatory. None of my edicts are, but I strongly encourage you not to hesitate the next time he forgets your anniversary or doesn't clean the dishes after you cooked. I mean you slave away for three hours on Zucchini Alfredo, all by yourself with no help from the cooks or the maids and he just sips his beer and—

Sorry, I got carried away. Ah, whatever I don't need to erase I'm Taylor freaking Swift.

Anyway, inside the brochure is an outline of the agenda and activities we offer at these camps. This is Taylor Swift, and you better have a good day!!!

Love,
Taylor

"Jesus, huh?" Mr. Bennett asked her. "These are old too. No swiftie would be able to read this now."

"Can you leave me alone?" Leigh asked. There was another picture of men knitting and bowing to a Taylor Swift cardboard cutout.

"Leigh." Mr. Bennett looked as if he was going to say something more, but then he just said, "Fine."

Leigh tossed the brochure over her shoulder, disgusted.

By the time they made it past the highway overpass, Leigh had realized Evan was missing. She asked everyone around her, but most of them didn't know who she was talking about.

Martha had to snap Leigh out of it. "Focus, Leigh."

"But Evan, he's—"

"Forget Evan. We need you! Look." Martha pointed to her left ankle. Leigh realized it was bleeding out under a shirt used as a crude bandage. "If he's on the other end of this formation or watching his last sunset on someone's lawn, he wants to believe we're going to do this. He wants to know you're going to survive this day and get us to where we need to be. The old world didn't work great, but it's sure as hell of a lot better than this."

Leigh wanted so badly to react to Evan's vanishing (she put it in such terms to minimize the pain) by crying. But she'd seen too much that morning. That feeling changed as her group, at last, reached the rendezvous point. It was a massive parking lot outside of the Tayloradium. In the distance, Leigh saw the structure. A sign was lit up and said "Swifta-Cola." The spaces were mostly empty, but there were signs of Katy's big distraction. Before Leigh could get a better look at it, Maura nearly tackled her with a hug.

"You're okay!" Leigh rejoiced. Maura's hair was re-colored, this time, blue.

"Yes," said Maura. "Just fine. Good to see you too. Listen, we have everyone else pushing ahead so it's a bit smoother for us on the final stretch. The swifties are dropping like flies, but they still have numbers on their side. Not hard to wonder how the fuck swifties took over in the first place."

"They got the president early on," said Mr. Bennett.

"Yeah." To Leigh, she said, "Before we go, there's someone who needs to see you."

"Huh?" Leigh asked.

Leigh was taken across the street. The pavement was torn apart, and there were small fires with buildings in disrepair. Then she saw a woman being dragged by her hair, screaming and protesting.

"Who is that?" Leigh asked Maura. "This isn't—"

"No. Close. That's Siobhan Mallory. Taylor's second-in-command. President of the Taylor Swift Fan Club. She was left as a human in order to remain lucid. She's informed us that for the first time in years, there was an order directly from Taylor herself to turn off the speakers all across the city."

"We thought so," said Martha.

"Why?" asked one of the women guarding Leigh.

"I guess because they're so few humans left in the world, Taylor isn't as interested in conversion into her fold anymore. She just wants us dead as quickly as possible. So yeah. Take no prisoners, basically."

"Taylor must have known we'd have defenses against the speakers, so she took them entirely off the table in favor of sacrificing some of her own fans," another guard, a man commented. "Sick bitch."

"I say it's a decisive move, given her position," admitted Maura.

Leigh stopped paying attention to the conversation as she took in all the devastation around her. It smelled like sulfur, and there were piles upon piles of old firework canisters and wrappers. There were also vehicles, one of which had a ceramic lion's head at its mast. The vehicle itself had crashed into a building, so the head was tilted to the side. Most of all, there were bodies. Some on their backs, some squirming, some chanting their culling songs courtesy of Taylor Swift.

"What happened here, Maura?"

Maura turned her gaze to a streetpost where Katy sat up rubbing her bloody face.

"Katy!" Leigh cried out. She knelt to see her. Katy's arms were pressed against her own chest, holding her collapsed body.

"She doesn't have long," said Maura.

"Neither do we," said Martha. "Trouble's on its way."

She looked off to the way they had come.

"Do it, Leigh," Katy said.

"What?"

"Rub this blood off of my face. It's gross. Take it for the rest of your journey. I can't believe you made it this far. I'm so proud of you, Leigh."

"She's disoriented," explained Maura. "We won this battle, but if we don't patch those speakers fast, we're going to be overwhelmed."

Martha's words on Evan echoed within Leigh, and she understood. Doing as Katy commanded, she wiped the blood from her mentor's face with her sleeves.

"Leigh, I don't think she really meant to do that, honey," said Maura.

"Taylor's got a few redeemable songs, you know?" said Katy. "They're something everyone can enjoy, even with the lack of substance argument. But here's where it goes wrong. You can't set yourself up as a metric for society to judge themselves against. All of us pop stars, we are completely numb to the suffering that goes on. We just put on a good show as a distraction and the people went nuts. The fucking media, though. Geez. I never had it out with Taylor Swift. Not back then. The magazines were just trying to sell papers. This was my last show, and I really gave it to them. Like walking into it all on an animatronic lion. Everyone told me it was so evocative, but I never knew the feeling myself, being up there. We didn't have any heavy artillery, so we used all the fireworks we could carry. What a great send off. But that isn't what's important here." Katy's eyes shuttered and she blinked several times. Then she vomited. Some of it got on Leigh, but she didn't care. She waited for what Katy had to say. "You're what's important. The present. The next step. The one who tells people they need to be themselves again."

"I don't want to be worshiped. Don't worry," said Leigh.

"It doesn't matter what you want. The people create

their own image of you. What did I just say about the media?"

"So what do I do?" asked Leigh.

"Uhh, worry about that after you've got people to worry about."

"Katy!"

"No, Leigh. I've shown you everything I can."

"Tell her what she needs to know, so we can get out of here. Jesus, Katy," said Maura.

"She doesn't have the answers," said someone from behind them.

"Evan, you made it!" said Maura. She threw her arms around him gently.

"Why aren't you running?" he asked them.

Katy began wheezing between her words. "I'm not sorry you hate me. It just contributed to our victory. I don't get to see it, but I needed to see you. It was selfish, but I am Katy Perry, you know. Eh, that's just what the religion jerks called me after I stopped singing gospel. Selfish, yeah whatever. Did I ever tell you I used to be a gospel singer? Go finish this, Leigh." Katy blinked a few times, then her eyelids remained still.

As Leigh nodded, she felt the lump in her throat constrict. Holding it in as best she could, whoever could still stand up left the parking lot behind with another legion of swifties giving them chase.

ELEVEN

Katy had been right. Taylor never anticipated this strategy from her enemies, the ones who were being systematically phased out by what she mistakenly considered to be some Darwinian principle.

Putting limited defenses up on the speaker hubs at the Tayloradium, Leigh's group made it in successfully. The swifties guarding the booth had no idea what was happening as the human forces pummeled them into a decisive defeat. Maura appropriated their walkie-talkies.

With their plan unfolding, it seemed Taylor was sending all available swiftie forces to the Tayloradium to stop whatever was happening.

As Leigh looked out through the window of the broadcasting room, the swifties were coming by numbers, the magnitude of which caused Martha to become vociferous as she asked again, "How much longer will it take, Tim?"

Tim was Katy's other sound engineer, who also had a hand in crafting the tracks they were trying to patch into Nashville's speaker system. Ralph was there tinkering on a computer, refusing to be disturbed. "Not longer than an hour, but it's kind of hard to tell like this. Look, instead of standing over my shoulder, can you guard the door? Maybe find a microphone for Leigh to use or something?"

"On it," said Evan. He left the sound panel with Mr. Bennett, Dale, and some others to search the closet nearby. "Cleaning supplies, hat. Shit."

"Ah, sweet," said Maura, who found some more walkie-talkies. "We're in good shape, I'd say. Look, I say we all spread out to find a mic. Who's in?"

"Me," said Leigh.

"You need to stay here," said Martha. "The swifties are already pouring in. We can't expose you."

"Martha, wow, really?" asked Maura. "Taylor's going to focus her troops to this location. Why else would we be here?"

An argument ensued, culminating in a victory for Maura when swifties began running down the hallway with apparent orders to liberate the speaker hub from enemy control.

"Okay, we get it. You're right," said Martha. "What now?"

"We can't let them get in, Martha," said Maura.

"Duh, but what about the others? If they found a microphone, they're probably stuck."

"What a fucking mess," said Maura, as a bullet zipped through the glass on the door and sent the shards flying too close for comfort.

Despite all the pressure on her and the imminent threat of death, all Leigh could feel was her empty stomach. Instead of eating an old probably rotten granola bar, she looked over the lyrics to one of the songs she'd written while the others returned fire. She'd be singing the song soon. Could it really be powerful enough to save them all?

Their group splintered off once more. Ten people stayed with Tim and Ralph in the broadcasting studio while the remaining twelve with Leigh at the center fought their way to a stairwell in search of Evan and the others. But deciding it was unlikely they had left the floor, they doubled-back to find Evan, Dale, and the others cornered by swifties. Leigh's group saved them, and they returned to the broadcasting room as Evan had found several microphones.

"They got Mr. Bennett though," said Dale.

Leigh remembered how the old man had saved her awhile back. She remembered how he'd bug her with his insistence on teaching her things she'd be learning in school if there still was an education system. Mr. Bennett was kind. But perhaps it was for the wrong reasons. Leigh was glad he was gone, so why did she feel pain? He'd never tried to do anything to her. Part of Leigh felt it just wasn't in the man's nature.

"Leigh, get it together. We have a microphone," said Martha.

"Shit, it's detective," said Evan, meaning defective. He cursed at his mistake. The fatigue set within him so much that he told the others, "I've gone as far as I can right now. I'll stay and guard the sound guys over here."

"Evan, just sit tight," said Maura. "You did good. No one expects more from you. We'll have this taken care of in a jiffy."

With Tim and Ralph in the final stages of preparation for Leigh's set, they found a wireless microphone that was synced up with the equipment.

"Let's all make for the stage," said Maura.

"We're going to do this out in the open?" asked Martha.

"Look, Martha, either the recordings are going to work or not," said Maura. "We're going all in. The swifties are being told to go for the speaker hubs, not the stage. If we get there first and start things, they'll at least stop and listen to whatever is going on with the speakers, Taylor or not."

"It's what we all signed up for," said Leigh.

"Besides, Ralph still needs to coordinate the equipment backstage with the speaker hubs here," said Tim.

At last, Ralph surfaced from the computer. "Now that we're done here, you set things up down there."

There was a pounding sound coming from the broken door outside of the broadcasting room. "It's Liam. I need help."

"I thought you said he was gone," Maura said to Dale.

"Yes. He's been… compromised. They tried changing him."

Liam entered. "They got me." The spot where his

earlobe had once been was bleeding. Turning towards Leigh, he said, "But Leigh. God, I just—" Coming in closer, Mr. Bennett raised his arms up, slowly approaching.

"No!" Leigh raised the Glock. Mr. Bennett did not stop. The Taylor Swift lyrics began forming from his lips. Leigh shot once, aiming at the old man's head but before that, Maura's bullet hit him in the side.

"More coming," said Mr. Bennett before he died.

Something about seeing Mr. Bennett bleed out caused Maura to freak out. "But I got the scholarship. I got it." Maura kept repeating that. She tossed her piece across her head and kneeled, and then her hands started rubbing her head.

"Great, now Maura's done too," said Martha.

"She's snapped," said Evan. "I'll watch over her."

"You need to watch for the swifties, Evan," said Martha. "What's more important?"

"Getting Maura back," said Leigh. "I'm not leaving her behind too!" She forced Maura onto her feet and doused her with water. Maura's breathing became irregular, and she let out a scream.

"Let's go!" Maura said.

"Oh fuck," said Leigh.

And like that, they were racing to the center of the Tayloradium, obliterating swiftie after swiftie until their ammunition became scarce. In response, they tried to take every gun from the swifties, but even that tactic couldn't compensate for the sheer number of additional swifties on pursuit of them. Maura gradually came back to her senses. She did not let go of her gun again. They touched the green of the stadium. It was packed with swifties. On the bleachers, on the green, everywhere.

"Time for another sprint, y'all," said Maura.

Leigh was with Maura, Dale, and five others, none of which Leigh knew. They had fled from the stage at the center of the stadium to an executive box at the other end of where they had entered the field. The sound engineers were, hopefully, wrapping things up. But as Leigh watched the swifties swarming the stages, she had no illusions of their situation. There were swifties trying to enter the box from the door inside and from the opening they'd made in the glass. Trays and other crude objects in the executive box were propped up against the aperture to repel the swifties, but barricade they'd made in a pinch was coming apart.

"What do we do?" Leigh pressed Maura.

"We still have to wait, hun," said Maura.

"What if they get in?"

"Well, it was a good run."

"No, hell no," said one of the others, a young man with an unkempt beard. "I don't like that. I say we—"

A bullet flew into the box, and he was interrupted as he ducked. So they waited, feeling their failure. Leigh realized the swifties on the other side of the door were setting fire to the corridor.

"Scorched earth," said Maura. "Goddammit. We're pinned again."

Not long after, they left the box through a smashed glass window and jumped onto the bleachers, and the swifties followed. The pursuit didn't last long, and they were running as high up as they could get. They were down to one full magazine left in a Beretta. The young man was wrestling Maura for it, in denial and not wanting to die.

The speakers came on. It was Katy Perry's recording doing her best Taylor Swift impression. "Hello, loves. Please pause your attacks and listen to your new leader, Leigh. I've totally been getting her ready under the radar to become the new me. She's awesome, give her a chance, guys… I love you."

That was followed by Leigh's recording of "Blank Space." It was being played throughout the city. Through all the radio stations. Perhaps not even just Nashville.

The swifties paused, not understanding what was happening. This was the first song they'd heard in a very long time that wasn't Taylor Swift, even if it was a Taylor Swift song. The song was rerecorded and had been replaced with acoustic instruments, such as piano and guitar. Leigh listened to herself, embarrassed, and knew she had to take the microphone and sing her songs next. The Taylor Swift song mollified their enemies. They did not chase after Leigh and the others.

Leigh imagined a dying Mr. Bennett singing along to the recording.

"It's almost time for your song!" Dale exclaimed.

The swifties resumed trying to finish them as the last verse was leading into the bridge of "Blank Space." Leigh watched as Maura raced to protect her.

The speakers went silent for two seconds, and then cued up again with the instrumental introduction to Leigh's song, cuing up her live vocal performance. Raising the microphone to her mouth, Leigh's last chance arrived.

"Meager"

Lyrics by Leigh Flanagan

[Refrain]
Meager people
Placed in silence
Destitute fate
Constant violence

Meager portions
Long gone icing
Loving small things
Living's righteous

[Verse]
Capable,
Deserved, like-minded
The slaves of song
A sickly bond

I could be safe
If I hid out
But I'll reveal
What's truly flawed

I love you all

[Refrain]
Meager people
Placed in silence
Destitute fate
Constant violence

[Verse]
Come along,
Take back your hearts
Be on your own,
Give away your wants

We could be
A society
With fair treatment
Equality

[Refrain]
Meager people
Placed in silence
Destitute fate
Constant violence

[Outro]

I love you all
& you & you
& you & you

I love you all
& you & you
& you & you

TWELVE

Missing a few lines toward the start of her song, Leigh had felt herself slip almost entirely into the perception that the swifties would converge upon her and eviscerate her for the heresy of breaking one of the Swift edicts. And as she grew closer and closer to the end of her last song with the microphone close to her mouth, she saw both the swifties and some humans, watching, wondering how each would react. Before Leigh was done, however, a massive fanfare entered from a lower partition and started marching towards the stage that had been erected there.

Leigh did not stop, even though she knew who that procession was bringing in. With their paltry numbers there was no way they'd be able to bring her down. So Leigh just continued to sing, as it seemed to slow time all around her. Was her performance that captivating?

Everyone's attention was shifting from Leigh to Taylor's congregation, which stopped. Leigh had only heard descriptions of Taylor Swift before, and they did not do justice as Leigh spotted her. She was a beautiful woman, but certainly not a girl as the others had remembered her as. Years had passed, and her age showed. Her wavy locks of hair seemed to have a shade of gray, but Leigh couldn't confirm it as far away as she was.

Taylor suddenly turned her head and looked at Leigh, the ruler's glittering dress sending twinkles, a lurid shine in all directions, promising to dominate all they could touch. She was handed a microphone. When Leigh was finished with her song, Taylor Swift clapped. Twice. The woman formed a silly smile with her lips that grew until her face was stretched.

"Come here. Come to me, hun! Yeah, you baby. Come on down!" Taylor spoke with a startling firmness into the microphone.

The swifties stood by, poised to capture her. Leigh shook her head in refusal. Maura and the others stood around her. The Beretta was out of ammo.

"Come alone or be taken!" Taylor commanded.

"They're still ready to follow Taylor, kid," Maura said.

"I think this is the end of the road," Dale said.

"I don't want to face her," Leigh said.

"I'm sorry," Maura said."We'll fight until we drop. That's our last option. What the fuck were we thinking? The fucking ocean!" She beat her fists into her head, unraveling them so that the fingernails scraped down the sides of her face. "Zachary!" Then she raised her fists as more the swifties began to surround them following a rapid succession of orders from Taylor Swift.

They backed up until the swifties were behind them too. No more moves against the swifties could be made. The circle around them closed in, rippled, and shrank until there was no space between them and the mass of swifties.

Leigh was in a cell, just waiting to die.

Why hadn't Taylor simply had them shot and killed right then and there? She had the power. The answers came a few days after they were taken into custody, by Taylor herself.

As a precaution, Leigh was restrained. Taylor Swift entered Leigh's cell, and at first, Leigh thought the woman was spouting lies. But then something about the genuine nature of Taylor's eyes cast doubt on that notion.

"You want to know what I think of your song?" Taylor asked with no preamble.

"I don't care," said Leigh. She would have had her arms crossed if they weren't already in a straight-jacket.

Taylor sat in a chair at a reasonable distance from Leigh,

as Leigh had developed a habit of spitting on anyone who got too close. "I thought it was like, so good. It has potential. Though it's nothing extraordinary itself."

"Fuck you," said Leigh, her lips twitching into a snarl.

"Leigh. Is that your real name? I'm going to, uh, tell you some things you don't want to hear. First, you are not going to die. I'm sorry. The second is, well," Taylor paused, seeming unsure of how to put it, "I want you to listen without any interruptions, do you understand?"

"Turning me into a swiftie then?"

"No, Leigh. I can only surmise that Katy's plan was to pass off those recordings you played through the city as a pseudo-symbolic gesture of me passing the baton of leader onto you. Is that about right?"

"Yeah. Sure. Whatever."

"I'm glad you aren't lying. See, my squad's already derived the truth from your friends."

Leigh became more interested in Taylor's words, practically jumping out of her chair from anticipation, though she was impeded by her restraints. "Are they okay?!"

"I promise to tell you, but you need to let me say what I'm going to say. Is that fair, dear?"

"Just go ahead. Act like you can't do whatever you want."

"I'm not a goddess, Leigh. I'm just me. People shouldn't have confused it. Even those of you who haven't been turned.

"So to begin, let me just say whatever you have been told about me, it's just a distorted perception. I'm a human being. I bleed. I have weaknesses, vulnerabilities, flaws. I gained fame, wealth, and then power. That changes a person. But Leigh, I never wanted this. I swear to God. We put out that ridiculous single, 'Even Without High Heels,' and I was so numb from the lifestyle I was living that I didn't even realize my body was starting to turn against me. My metabolism was slowing down, I was reaching an age where my friends were settling down and having kids. There is a point where an artist climaxes in their career. It has to happen. Where they reach critical mass. Then it's a downward. Down. I kept thinking that. Beginning, middle, end. Concept album. Greatest Hits record instead of new material. That's when this producer came to me and said he'd developed this strange, advanced beat, one that had evolved from all conventions of pop music dating back as far as there's been pop music. He said if I integrated it into my music before anyone else, my influence and popularity would be increased exponentially. I just wanted to set myself apart from the rest of the artists, and I'd exhausted all my creative juices over the years. I'm sure they were still there, but I…" Leigh remained rigidly stoic as Taylor began to tear up, "…thought it had something to do with my passage into… my thirties. I have used my music to heal myself, to escape from reality. To give people that same feeling. But what he did… he fooled me. Or maybe he had no idea.

"Next thing I knew, I was the reason for an entire coup d'état of all established governments globally. My face, my lyrics, my career was turned into a weapon to reconfigure things into something supposedly more to my pleasing. Soon, those affected didn't even know what they were doing, as you've seen. They just stare and wait to hear what I have to say, Leigh. I'm telling you, I didn't want this. It wasn't who I was. But when most of the world wants you to be their leader, their muse, it's… I made the best of a bad situation. I had that producer killed before the nature of his beats could be broken down and understood. If I was going to be the ruler of the entire world, I had to take precautions. What I'm saying is, I'm not some evil ego freak. It's just one shallow perception."

"So why are swifties so violent? Why the boyfriend reform camps? Why?" Leigh demanded.

"I got carried away. I didn't know what I was doing. They all just wanted to make me happy, and I knew if the world just embraced my music, it would be a utopia. But free will prevailed. Before I could pull it off, if I even could, it became this— a myopic culture of mindless zombies unable to function without my constant attention. I love them all, but Jesus, are they a burden. I cannot have one second to myself. It's awful.

"Leigh. I've failed. And I have resisted people like Katy trying to dispose of me all this time. But I'm tired, Leigh. And I'm telling you, this has gone too far. What I thought was if I could just get everyone turned into a swiftie, things would be fine. But no. I'm stepping down. Your plan has worked, but we have a long way to go. The first thing I'm going to do is remove the conditioning placed on the swifties, and as you planned. Then I will transfer my title to you." Taylor played with a pen in her hands.

"But Taylor, you're insane! I can't do these things. I don't want to become you. I just want the world to be safe. No more obsessive worship or hypnotic pop music."

"I will help you, Leigh. They will listen to you. You can teach them to stop the fighting, or you can teach them to think for themselves. You can't do it all, though. If you take my position and work to create peace, there's no free will. You just continue phasing out the remaining of those like you who are not hypnotized until there are none left but you. But if we bring those affected down from their mindless stupor of pop music hypnosis, there will be resistance and conflict akin to when I was installed on the throne."

"Katy told me, she said she thought every person deserved to be free, even if they did bad things with that freedom. That's why she fought so hard against you because you took that away."

"But it's not necessarily that one course of action is better than the other, Leigh. There are many gray areas, and the decision will ultimately be in your hands. And after you've made that decision, I will never speak again."

"What?"

"My words have caused too much confusion and destruction. My so-called power ripped me apart from my family who I couldn't even save in the madness. I lost my cat. From now on, my actions will show my true wishes."

"Taylor, why don't you just take responsibility for your mistakes instead of giving them to me?"

"You will try to make things better. You have the future." The blonde bangs across Taylor's forehead jumped outward for a moment as she looked away from Leigh. "Alone, I don't give two shits for anything in this world anymore."

Taylor Swift's address to her followers was coupled with new songs by Leigh employing the same technology Taylor had initially used, but for a different purpose. These songs became less and less catchy and hypnotic and became more and more lyrically potent (subject matter consisting of the issues facing them as a world), compelling, and meaningful. Eventually, the world desired to listen to music of this variety in favor of Taylor's hypnotic album. They, like Dale, became more rational. There was surprisingly little resistance amongst the swifties, perhaps due to Taylor's own endorsement of the shift back into a less savage form of government.

"I mean, come on, everyone. You haven't noticed, but my monthly albums have grown more and more pessimist to this whole set-up," Taylor explained at one summit. "I mean, I love you guys, but you need to think for yourself. And I know that sounds like an order, and that sort of undermines the message, but figure out for yourself why it's best to do so. I'm frankly tired of all the bloodshed in my name. Have you really not noticed these messages in my recent songs?"

The swifties stared back oblivious at first, but their recovering minds put the pieces together.

"Well, yeah. We should not be solely obsessed with art and creation when base survival has been such a problem. Once everyone in the world is able to survive and more, then we should direct our lives towards the decadence of artistic adoration, not before."

Leigh found great thinkers who'd worked for Taylor and from pockets of survivors who'd stayed in hiding avoiding the album's effects. Together, they drafted a series of plans meant to not only restore what once was, but to improve upon it, as Taylor had so horribly failed at.

Taylor indeed took her vow of silence but continued writing to Leigh, and they became very close to the point where eventually, Leigh's songs were heard first by Taylor.

The world found its balance once more, but there were still senseless killings. Dale was a spiritual guide for swifties trying to fully regain their humanity. Maura lost her life a year following the storming of Nashville while trying to neutralize a roving gang of nomadic swifties. Evan, on the other hand, survived his Lupus and started a family, and Leigh felt that balance settle within her as she mourned Maura. And Zachary. Everyone she'd lost. Even Trevor.

One evening, Leigh received a letter from Maura. It was dated a few weeks before her passing. It informed her of a message Mr. Bennett had entrusted her with. What it boiled down to, essentially, was an inquiry into Mr. Bennett's court case. The truth, he explained, could be found if she was able to find and ask the two girls who'd put up the molestation charges against him.

After obtaining court transcripts of the case, Leigh found she had a desire to seek out the plaintiffs involved— those who had been victimized by Mr. Bennett. Knowing she wanted to pay justice forward, she found them both alive on a farm in Indiana on a cold March morning. Leigh was still in a prominent position of power and wrestling with countless ethical dilemmas. It was made even worse when the two girls, Melinda and Olivia, confessed they'd made the entire molestation incident up. Mr. Bennett did not do it.

"Mr. Bennett, he just, ah, went on and on," said Bethany. "We were young."

"And stupid," said Melinda. "History. He taught history. He never touched us. We made it up because we thought he was a fucking boring asshole."

And what those girls didn't know that Leigh knew Mr. Bennett was a good man. And these girls were actually the true evil she'd perceived in him during Katy's rigorous training stemming from trauma. How to Make Art 101. The twisting in her mind she'd felt when she had believed that Mr. Bennett had actually raped these girls, it was all redirected to the liars she faced.

Endless echoes of justice pervaded her mind, and her fury intensified. Leigh felt like she could be the one to equalize things for Mr. Bennett. They'd treated him like shit and ruined his life for no reason. Leigh held their fates in her hands. She could dole out justice, change the world. Condemn evil or try to salvage it.

Suddenly, Leigh felt Taylor Swift was not so bad.

Dear Swifties,

I have no doubt some lines in here may be construed as offensive. On the surface of this satire, it seems as if I'm likening or reducing you to mindless zombies. That your favorite artist is an evil pop culture monster who embodies deadly ideals which threaten humanity's very existence. And worst of all that her music is bad.

These points, even if I believed them are subjective, and I think anyone who actually reads this story will understand the true message. Sadly, those who don't will probably not be present to read this clarification. Oh well, I agree with Katt Williams regarding the need for haters.

What I do think is an issue is the state popular music today. Money talks. A lot of acts today don't have to write quality music. It has to be catchy, that's more important than quality. The message can be hollow, the values can be immoral, and the passion of the artist can be utterly sucked out if it stands to compromise sales potential. I don't refer to Taylor Swift in this instance, it is clear she loves what she does and her dreams have come true. In fact, she's somewhat ahead of the curve as she writes a lot of her own music and lyrics. However, I do think there is something wrong with the media shoving certain music down our throats until we have to tolerate it simply because it's on the radio fifty times a day.

That's not how art should be enjoyed. We should take this further into consideration because most people listening to Top 40 are catch up in how it sounds, not what is being said, and definitely not what it means. The result is a subconscious influence in which this music defines us as a collective culture.

It became necessary for me in the course of writing this work to listen to and analyze Taylor Swift's music. I listened to every song I could find. There were some I have come to genuinely enjoy.

As the colossus major labels relying further and further on appearance over substance in their artists, fortunately one has alternatives in this day and age. But even so, there is no escaping the potential consequences when pop music is what the majority of the population is exclusively exposed to.

Like I said, the media produces influence. Talented artists (not with something *superior* to contribute to music than Taylor Swift, but something just as worthy of being heard) are ignored. On television, music is judged now. They set a metric of arbitrary criterion. Almost always originality is excluded from this criterion.

Originality is what I'm calling for. Of course we can appreciate when a singer is outstanding and just brings a new evocation to a song like "Hallelujah", but there should be more value in a performer having that aesthetic with his own words. And a song, a performance should not be judged relative to another. It doesn't always have to be a competition.

And as you can see, there are multiple incarnations of Taylor Swift. There's the Taylor Swift the media tells us about (this is the Taylor media-self I portrayed, and in turn contribute to this fallacious perception of Taylor Swift), there's what we formed of her from our own perceptions, then there is Taylor herself. Just another person. If you want to get it even more convoluted, I could question in which of Taylor's song is she the actual speaker?

But it is time to digress. These myriad folds detract from a fact I hope you will consider. Ultimately, we must place Taylor Swift and every other thing we are ostensibly forced to listen to in the proper context.

Stay gorgeous,
Ryan Starbloak

Thank you SO MUCH for reading this book!!!

If you enjoyed it, I do hope you'll leave a review on this book's Amazon page. As an indie author, I cannot understate the importance of reviews. They pretty much determine whether or not I can continue producing more content and get it out to you in an orderly fashion. On top of that, they allow me to improve the way I do things and create even greater stories. If you're interested in receiving a free review copy of any of my other titles, leave an honest review for this book where you purchased it. Send a link of your review to ryansleavittscifi@gmail.com. I'll smile, and send the next book of your choice right over!

I have a lot of interesting stuff coming soon. You can sign-up for my newsletter at:

www.ryansleavitt.com

Earth is gone… humanity is not.

A cutting-edge sci-fi serial about the desperate preservation of life, consciousness, and love in the wake of Earth's end.

Is it worse to learn or not to know?

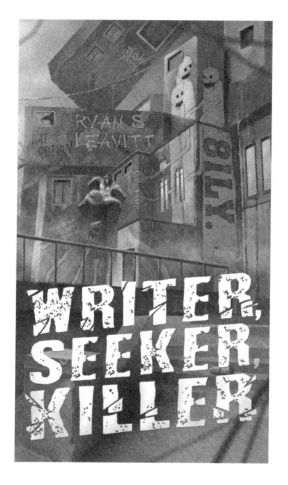

A psychological thriller set in New Orleans
dealing with the failure of the War on Drugs
and a search for the metaphysical.

About the Author

Ryan Starbloak is an author, who also writes under the name Ryan S. Leavitt. His books have been featured on BookBub and he has also appeared on the briefly televised reality sitcom *Quiet Desperation*. He currently lives in New Orleans, where he also performs in the bands Allision and The Every Year.

Instagram: @theeveryyear
Youtube: Ryan S. Leavitt
Music: allision.bandcamp.com
theeveryyear.bandcamp.com